the whip hand

stories

First published 2016 by
FREMANTLE PRESS
25 Quarry Street, Fremantle WA 6160
(PO Box 158, North Fremantle WA 6159)
www.fremantlepress.com.au

Consultant editor Naama Amram
Cover design Carolyn Brown, www.tendeersigh.com.au
Cover photograph www.shutterstock.com: jujikrivne

 A catalogue record for this
book is available from the
National Library of Australia

ISBN: 9781925164152 (paperback)
ISBN: 9781925164183 (ebook)

Fremantle Press is supported by the Western Australian State
Government through the Department of Cultural Industries,
Tourism and Sport.

Publication of this title was assisted by the Commonwealth
Government through Creative Australia, its arts funding and
advisory body.

the whip hand

stories

MIHAELA NICOLESCU | NADINE BROWNE

 FREMANTLE PRESS

Contents

Contents

The Returning

Mihaela Nicolescu

Contents

Gone, Baby, Gone

They slowed down just outside Watford and pulled into an empty McDonald's parking lot. Erika sat holding the steering wheel, the engine still running, her hands cold, until something tugged at her sleeve.

'What are we doing here?' the kid asked.

'We're resting,' Erika said, grabbing her jacket and bag from the back seat. Erika got out of the car and waited, but the little girl did not budge, just watched Erika with mild cow eyes.

'For fuck's sake ...' Erika walked over to the passenger's seat and pulled open the door. 'Will you get out please,' she said.

'I want to go home,' the little girl said. She sat staring dead ahead, her arms crossed tightly, her little round spectacles fogged up by her own breath. She was still wearing the pink Barbie-themed pyjamas.

'You don't want a Happy Meal, then?' Erika said, and saw the girl's gaze flash towards the restaurant, stopping for a moment on the playground outside.

Erika followed her gaze.

A merry-go-round, a couple of swings and a set of monkey bars. All in bright paints, all looking sad and abandoned, all looking garish and pointless.

'You can play afterwards if you want,' she offered.

The girl gave a great sigh, and made to release her seatbelt. She struggled with the buckle, her clumsy hands not able to unfasten it, but when Erika tried to reach over to help, the brat swatted her aside and snapped:

'I can do it myself!'

Erika took a step back, then another, and turned away.

'Forget you,' she said over her shoulder.

'Wait! Wait! You can't leave me ...' the voice rose to a shrill that seemed to cut into the base of Erika's skull.

She continued towards the entrance, ignoring the screaming, and stepped into the warm, bright McDonald's embrace. At the counter she ordered two coffees, two cheeseburgers and a Happy Meal.

As she was paying, she heard the door open and close, and little feet scuttle to her side.

'You can't do that!' the girl said, loudly. She looked like she was going to cry.

'Be quiet please,' Erika said, without looking down.

'You can't just leave kids in cars ... Don't you know anything? Huh? You can't just ...'

'Shut up. And if you start crying, I'm leaving your whiny arse here,' Erika said, and was immediately sorry. She smiled apologetically to the boy who handed her the paper bags.

'Here,' she gave the kid the Happy Meal box, 'go and sit down.'

Erika took her change and smiled again at the boy.

'My sister,' she told him.

He nodded. Erika thought she could see judgement in his eyes, under the brim of his cap.

At a corner table, Erika kicked off her heels. The kid was unpacking her Happy Meal. She lined up the burger, chips and drink, her lips moving, her face animated. She mumbled, 'So that's what you have to do ...' pushed her glasses further up and bounced an ugly stuffed dinosaur up and down on the table.

The kid unwrapped her burger and took a nibble. Erika watched. She took tiny, quick bites, then scrunched up her face.

'I'm a hamster, look,' she said.

'Yeah, that's great,' Erika tried to smile.

The kid looked up shyly between hamster nibbles.

'You're very pretty,' she told Erika, and Erika felt herself harden to the compliment.

'Just eat your food and let me think.'

The girl blinked, wounded, and Erika tried to think of something kind to say, but she could not, and so she thought of other things instead.

She was six or seven years old and out shopping with her mother.

Erika had been a beautiful child. Big blue eyes, chestnut ringlets; a gorgeous little thing, a poppet, a doll. Her mother would look at her in disbelief and say to her friends, 'Look at this child. Where did she come from? Where did all this luck come from?'

And one day Erika was out shopping in Tesco with her mum. It was early in the morning and before either of them knew how it had happened, Erika was throwing a tantrum in the confectionery isle.

An old lady stopped by the commotion and told Erika, very gently, to be a big girl and to listen to her mummy. No, chocolate wasn't good for little girls, and wasn't it a shame to cry when she'd be so pretty if she smiled.

Hearing this broke her mum's paralysis. She plunged down next to them and took Erika by the arms. Looking straight at Erika, she said, 'She's a spoilt, ugly little thing on the inside, a little black lump on the inside.'

Erika fell silent, her cheeks glazed with tears, snot running into her mouth. Her mother grabbed her hand and dragged her out of the supermarket, leaving their basket on the floor and the old lady staring after them.

Erika now looked out of the walls of glass, and thought for a moment that she saw a flash of blue and white in the distance. She sat up straight. Quickly she shoved her feet back into her shoes.

'Come on, you can eat that on the way.'

She grabbed the kid by the arm and pulled her outside.

The parking lot was still empty, but for her car, and as she was buckling the kid into the passenger's seat, she remembered that she had promised her a turn in the playground. This is how it begins, Erika thought. This is the start of the lie that leads to all the hate.

'I'm sorry,' she said, but the kid wasn't listening.

Erika got into the car and took out her mobile. She had eighteen missed calls and five messages. She took out a spliff from the bottom of her bag and lit up. God knows how long it had been there. It tasted of dirt and perfume, and Erika coughed between drags.

'Smoking is bad.'

Erika jumped, banging her head against the window; she had forgotten the kid.

Now she remembered.

She pulled the car back out onto the road, turned on the radio and, while pretending to listen to the news update, tried to think up a plan.

Maybe they could stay with Oli and his flatmates.

Oh yes, there was bound to be a party at Oli's and she needed a drink so badly right about now. She heard a rustle by her side and turned to see the kid fiddle with the radio.

Oh right. The kid.

Oh fuck.

'Where we going, Erika?' the girl asked.

'On holiday.'

'Are you crying, Erika?'

'No.'

'Here ...' the kid shoved her half-eaten hamburger in Erika's face, 'Nana says eating makes people happy.'

'Your grandmother doesn't know shit about making people happy.'

Erika had left home at fifteen after getting in early one morning, still buzzing, stinking of cigarettes and booze.

The usual hypotheticals followed: Have you no shame? What are you doing with your life? Where did I go wrong?

Erika had stopped on her way up the stairs and had stood swaying, looking at her mother. She told her, in a slur, how she had never felt this joyless hole to be her home; had never felt anything but a blank where maternal affection should have slotted in.

'You're drunk, it's disgusting. Go to bed,' her mother had said and tried to walk away, but Erika had clung onto her, pulling at her flannel nightgown, screaming, 'I fucking hate you, I fucking hate you.'

She did not speak to her mother for two years.

'Is she ... nice to you?' Erika asked the kid. She realised she was driving too fast and, pulling into the slow lane, asked again, 'Is Grandma nice to you?'

The kid drew a lopsided star in her breath on the window, and said, 'Yeah ...'

'You don't have to lie to me.'

'I know.'

'Does she play with you?'

'Yeah ...'

'Does she tell you you're pretty?'

The kid frowned. 'I don't know...'

'Does she say that you're a little doll, a little perfect doll? Does she look at you like she can't bear to see you?'

The kid stared blankly, her eyes huge and calm behind the pink wire frames, as if she knew more than she possibly could, as if she trusted in Erika more than she ever should. She wiped the star off the window, breathed and drew a heart instead.

'You know hearts mean *I love you*?'

'Yeah, I know.'

'Erika?'

'Yeah ...'

'Where are we going?'

Erika did not remember much about those two years.

She did remember the day she had crawled back to her mother's house. She had nowhere else to go. She had not planned for this. Erika knew that she could easily solve the problem by a visit to the clinic, a procedure many of her friends said was quick and simple and really no big deal, but she was already fifteen weeks on, and she could cup her belly in her hands and imagine a life.

So Erika went back home and, full of resentment, she named the baby Lilly, the name chosen by her mother. But to Erika it was never Lilly; it was *It* or *The Kid* or *Sweetheart*, but never Lilly.

She held it like a sack of potatoes. Read it stories. Took her for walks, holding her tiny hand.

Erika was always saying goodbye.

She was always going, gone, baby, gone, only to return weeks, sometimes months, later, bringing presents and guilt wrapped up in bright paper and tied up with ribbons.

For six years, Erika did not feel like anyone's mother.

For six years, Erika watched her own mother sprout

affection in a place that had been barren. Erika watched her mother and her daughter play together in the garden of her childhood home, making memories that should have been hers.

'It really is too bad this girl will grow up with no father,' her mother had said once.

'I grew up without a dad,' Erika had replied.

'That's not true, you had a dad. He died, but you had one.'

'Well, she had a father and he is dead too.'

'He is ...'

'He is fucking dead to me and to her. He's dead to us, right,' Erika said, louder than she'd meant to.

For six years, Erika was on her own, and then one day she thought about the way the kid would put up her arms to be picked up and fall into hysterical giggle fits when she was tired. She thought about the little frames around her eyes, and about eyes that were not spectacular but calm and mild.

Erika told a stranger at some party how she had a daughter, and when the stranger did not believe her, she wondered if it was really true, so she left the party and drove to her mother's house to make sure.

'What's wrong?' her mother had opened the door, bleary-eyed with sleep. 'Are you drunk? Jesus Christ, Erika, you're drunk.'

She stepped inside, expecting Erika to follow, but Erika did not move.

'I want her back,' Erika said.

Her mother turned to face her, looking brittle, the sleep now vanished from her eyes. She did not seem surprised, but told Erika to be serious. She told Erika to think about the child and be reasonable.

'I want her back,' Erika said again.

Erika stepped inside and rushed up the stairs, her mother following behind, urging her to not be foolish, to not wake the baby in the middle of the night. Outside the kid's bedroom, her anger shattered into desperation.

'Please don't do this ... She needs me, she needs me. Oh God please ... I'm phoning the police,' and she stumbled off to her own bedroom.

Erika crept into the kid's room and gently woke her, smoothing her hair and saying 'sweetheart' again and again. The kid blinked a few times, confused and, on seeing Erika, smiled and touched her face. In moments she was wide awake and reaching for her glasses.

'We're going on a trip,' Erika said and lifted her.

And now she was driving in the slow lane with the kid asleep in the passenger's seat, her mouth open and her glasses askew.

What had she thought?

Had she thought there'd be a place for them? That they'd wake up together in the mornings and Erika would make breakfast? Scrambled eggs and pancakes? That she'd lead the kid by the hand up pleasant hills to school, two little steps in black patent shoes for every one of Erika's.

The kid stirred in her sleep, and Erika remembered her own mother making pancakes and smiling, calling her 'baby'.

'Lilly...' Erika whispered, 'Lilly...'

Lilly opened her eyes and looked at her, and Erika knew that another goodbye was coming, but this time not because she was nobody's mother.

866

Mrs Copland say I must write journal to practise English. She say it good to write every day. She say it help us think more English. I ask if it help us think Australian and she smile. She smile only with her lips. Her eyes cold and far away like rocks on bottom of river.

I live with Mr Omar and wife in Perth. Wife is maybe thirty-five. She only five year older but she talk to me like you talk to little child.

I sleep in room with boxes. From my window I see neighbour house. Neighbour is Mr Cole. Every morning Mr Cole squeeze big belly into small car and drive to work. Mrs Cole try to make grass grow. All day she in garden with pink gloves looking after sand. Sometime when she see me she nod head. Mr Cole always shake head when he see me. He shake head and say 'damn reffos' or he shake head and stare at me with lips curled like angry dog.

Mr and Mrs Cole have daughter. They call her Georgie and she fourteen or fifteen year old. She smoke cigarettes and tell mother to go to hell. Every night I see her jump out of bedroom window. She come back early morning and sometime a boy come back with her and they stand outside window and hug and kiss. They stand for long time and boy always say 'stay a bit longer, you don't have to go' and she say that she have to go because her mum check on her in the morning. Then boy help her jump up on plastic table and back into house.

I ask Mrs Copland why kids talk bad and act bad and she tell me not to worry about that. She tell me I not understand English to know bad. I learn English when I little child, I say. I read poem and newspaper with my father. Mrs Copland smile and say 'sweetheart, I am trying to help you people'.

Mrs Copland call everyone 'sweetheart' but she not look at me when she say it and I feel like she telling lie. I talk with Somali lady in class and she say yes, yes, they do that here. They smile with cold eyes and they say 'love' and 'darling' with voice but not with heart. Lady hold my hand when she talk and she tell me about her baby back home. She ask me about my home and I tell her it here. She laugh and say no, no, this not your home, this home for Australian people or English people, people with white skin from cold countries, people who go to beach and listen to boom-boom-boom music, people who speak proper, and people who know other people who speak proper.

Maybe I between homes. My mother home is dust. It used to be big house, with blue tiles in yard and many flowers. It used to be full of cousins and aunties and uncles and everyone laughing and eating and talking. People always come to my mother house and they drink tea with my father, and they pray together and talk this and that together. Mother tell father to be quiet with this and that. She say to him to whisper this and that. But he say it wrong to not speak. He say we great people and great people must know to speak and think. He not scared. He talk this and that until I wake up with little sister crying and shaking me and saying 'komak, komak, someone break door'. And I take little sister in arms and run out into night and rocks hurt my feet like glass but I run and run to hills and stay there until morning time. And when morning come my mother home dust. It still there and garden still there, but my mother and father dead and my brothers arrested. My auntie not let me inside but her dress and hands and feet covered in blood and I get down on knees and kiss her feet and I not hear anything and not remember anything.

I not want home that is dust. I not want home that blow away in wind and wash away in rain. I want strong home. I want Australian home. I want to speak proper so I can speak not proper. I want to listen to boom-boom-boom music and go to beach and burn meat.

I live with friend of uncle and his wife but it not home. I meet them first time when I come off boat. My uncle say I must get on boat and go to Australia. He say it safe and there many jobs. When I meet wife I say salaam but she say to speak English. She speak like God pour honey in her mouth. She speak soft and her hands soft like baby skin and very beautiful. She ask me what I can do and I tell her I work in school at home. She ask if I want to be useful and I say yes, yes, of course. So I clean and cook for wife.

And I go to English class and learn to speak like honey.

And I write on pages for government to let me stay. I get form to write but not sure what it say. They say to read information carefully and I try but there many questions. There forty-five pages asking and telling and I not know difference. I ask Mrs Omar for help and she say 'yes, yes, another time'. She say 'yes, yes, another time' every time I ask. My uncle call me and he say I must fill out form. Uncle pay Mr Omar so I can learn to speak nice in community centre with Mrs Copland. Uncle say I must get visa or I like shadow. He ask Mr Omar to help me and Mr Omar ask Mrs Omar and Mrs Omar say 'yes, yes, another time'. And days go to weeks and to months and I cook and clean.

Every Monday afternoon I walk to community centre. One Monday after class I ask Mrs Copland what radiological report mean. She look at me with eyebrows up like someone scare her. I show her form and ask again. She say it mean something doctor do. I ask why and she take deep breath and tell me to go to Citizen Advice Bureau. I ask where I find this but she already out door. I hear her car start and she drive away very fast.

I walk home in dark. Night make any place feel like any other place. It nice to walk in dark with hot wind and sound of little animals. It feel like home. I take off shoes and walk barefoot. Uncle right. I am shadow. Maybe that why I feel happy in dark. During day I am nothing for people to see. During night I am like everything else.

When I get to Mr Omar street I smell cigarette and I see Georgie sitting on ground breathing smoke. She wear little dress and red lipstick and she look like woman but I know she child. She ask me what I stare at and I tell her I stare at her. She look at me like she confused. Then she ask me why I here, why I not go home. I tell her this is home and she say 'bullshit'. I ask why she speak so ugly and she swear at me. She stand up and throw cigarette away and walk off.

I go to Mr Omar house and Mrs Omar see bare feet and get angry. She tell me I dirty and I make her house dirty but she speak in our language. I smile because it so long I hear my language. Mrs Omar think I rude. I try explain hearing words in my language make me feel less like shadow. It like rain and I like grass and when it fall on me I grow. I feel like me when I had home. I feel like me at mother table with my brothers and sisters and cousins. I feel like me listening to father read stories his father read when he little child. Stories about prince and princess and about thieves and witches. There magic in father stories and I think for long time that magic save me but magic trapped in stories like bird in cage. Magic cannot save shadow. Only visa save shadow.

Mrs Omar look at me like I crazy and she call me 'silly girl'. She tell me to wash feet in garden. She tell me I hurry up and fix dinner because Mr Omar soon home. I wash feet and then I fix dinner and while I cook Mrs Omar watch TV show with singing. She watch with little smile on her lips like she dreaming sweet dream. Mrs Omar sit in big chair holding soft hands and she smile.

I stop ask Mrs Omar for help. I not write every day anymore. I forget when day and when night. I forget time. Time mean holiday or weekend or work for people but time not mean anything for me. People watch time and scared of time but I think time forget about me. It sweep over world in big wave and leave only me behind.

I take walk sometime. Sometime I watch cars on street and I jealous for people who have place to go. I jealous for people who in hurry. I walk very slow like old person and my mind go very slow. Everything around me go fast, fast, fast but I go more slow every day and I scared one day I will stop. Uncle not call me for many week and English class over now. I go for walk and I hope I meet Somali lady or other lady from English class but I know city very big and people very small.

One morning Mr Omar at work and Mrs Omar shopping so I alone in house. I sit in garden and watch sun move in sky. Then I hear loud noise. I look over wall between Mr

Omar house and Mr Cole house and I see Georgie bang on window. Window locked and she try to open. Her dress very dirty and she look like she fall down. She see me looking over wall and I think she going to scream at me but she look scared and she say 'Eric crashed his dad's car'. I ask if she hurt and she shake head. 'His dad's gonna kill us,' she say. She say car crash in trees and she walk home. I tell her to come to me and at first she look like she not want to, but then she stop pulling window and she come.

I take Georgie inside and I make tea. I give her dress to wear. It only dress I have and it big on little girl. She ask me this and that and I happy to talk. I hear my voice like stranger but the more I talk the more it sound like me. I tell her I try to get visa but it very hard. She look at me and say 'so you don't have visa' and I tell her I trying to get. Then I tell Georgie to call her mother and she does but she not happy. When Mrs Cole come to pick girl up she say that she lock window to teach Georgie lesson. Her face sour and she not look at me, not look at girl.

When Mrs Omar come home she talk with Mrs Cole quiet like they talk secret and then she come and she tell me I not stay in their house anymore. She say Mr Cole angry I took girl in house and that it not my business. She say Georgie told Mr Cole I not have visa and he want to call immigration and police and they not want trouble. I ask her where I go and she say it not her business.

At night Mr Omar come and he say I can stay. I ask what happen if Mr Cole call police and he say they send me away because I not have visa. I say that I try get visa but I need form and nobody help me. Mr Omar say he help me but I must be good and not make Mrs Omar angry.

I scared now. I scared that Mr Cole call police. Police maybe lock me in centre and everyone forget about shadow.

Police maybe send me back home but it not home anymore. Police send me to what was home long time ago like they send me to desert to find ocean. I scared and when I see Georgie I say 'please not call police, please tell father I not make trouble'. Georgie look at me like I not there and she tell me it better if I fuck off home. I not understand. Why everyone angry? Why nobody help? This country full and rich and people have everything and can say anything and do anything. People not understand that I want what they have but not what is their. I want home and family and job. But I not take their home and family and job.

When uncle call he speak with Mr Omar. Uncle angry because he give Mr Omar money to help me and Mr Omar not help. I ask uncle what I do and he say I get visa. I must get visa. When I get visa I not have to clean and cook for Mrs Omar. When I get visa police not send me away. After I talk to uncle I ask Mr Omar to help with papers. He say later.

I go to street and sit on ground. It dark but I sit with form and I try write. I sit for long time and I try understand. I not know block letters. I not know dependants. For first time in Australia I cry because I scared I never have home again. I cry like baby and I embarrassed but I cry and cry.

I hear sound and it make me jump. Georgie standing looking at me. She wearing big t-shirt and her feet bare. She look like she wake up from sleep. She look very much like little girl and I think about little sister. Georgie sit down next to me and ask why I cry. I say I sad and I scared. I say I need visa but nobody help me.

She ask why I not go back home but she not ask with ugly voice. She ask like child ask where rain come from. She ask like person who think home something everyone have like body. I tell her mother and father killed and it not safe in my country. She look at me and her eyes very big and she say 'that sucks'. Then she take papers from me and pen and she ask 'what's your name?' She ask 'do you have any dependants?' and when I say I not understand she say 'wait here' and run inside. She come back out with mobile phone and she look on phone and say 'do you have, like, kids or anything?'

She keep ask questions and write answers in neat writing like school teacher. I ask if it make her father angry if she help me but she keep writing and say 'whatever'. She say we go to immigration office tomorrow and that we go early. I say thank you, thank you and she say 'whatever'.

When I go in house again it late and I smile. Mrs Omar ask why I smile and where I been and why I not work.

I keep smile and I say 'whatever'.

Frozen

A long time ago, during our many summers on Grundvik Island, I would wake up early every Thursday and run down to wait for Jonas Ström and the mail.

I'd listen for his hoot in the pale light of morning, with the cool promise of a warm summer day climbing a horizon that surrounded me.

He'd approach, just a blue and red dot from where I stood, barefoot, worrying that Helena or Toma would find me and tease.

Then with a mighty honk he would pull up to the pier. Loud like Thor, tall and bright with a wide grin, he'd cast me in his shadow as he leaned down to hand me the newspapers and letters. He would say *'flicka lilla'*, little girl, *'du vaknar med fåglarna'*, you rise with the birds. Then, just as I'd prepare to open my mouth and say something, Helena and Toma would come tumbling down from the house, through the forest, and flank me, giggling, while the beautiful Jonas would be off with a final ear-splitting roar.

'You love him.'

'Mila is going to marry Mr Postman!'

And we would race up to the house, through the heavy oak front door that we joined forces to open, and into the kitchen where we collapsed in laughter at our mothers' feet.

We'd listen to their gossip until we were thrown out of the kitchen and into the sitting room, where our grandfather and my dad were locked in mortal combat over their backgammon board, brows furrowed, but conscious enough of the world outside their battle for my dad to mumble, 'Your daddy is winning this one, honey.' Grandfather would just smile, and wink, and tell me never to grow old. This is what he always told us kids and we'd nod solemnly, believing that we never would.

Outside, Toma's dad would be fixing something, hammering or sawing, and we'd stay well away.

By the afternoon everyone would leave the house and scatter. Our mums would sunbathe on the pier, while our dads would take the boat out, and we'd flash around the island.

***

On our final visit to Grundvik we had arrived in threes and fours, as always, in my uncle's motorboat. It was the middle of winter. We never came here at this time – Grundvik Island was the place of summer thrills – but our grandfather was turning eighty-five and we all gathered to celebrate.

Grundvik was a very different place.

In between the islands of the archipelago, the Baltic Sea lay in great sheaths of broken ice. Closer to the mainland ice-skaters were still venturing out, but here the currents kept the ice shifting, the waves pulling in and out of deserted beaches with black fingers.

Our island was abandoned to the wintry blues, covered in a blanket of pure white snow. Ancient pine and spruce swayed, green and lush, amid the black skeletons of oak, beech and maple. Here and there something stirred in the trees, scattering snow from the loaded branches. Then all was still again.

The mail boat still drifted by once a week, though it did not stop by the island. Its hoot could be heard somewhere far out, above the restless rumble, though it was soon drowned out by the sea and wind.

Summer dreams should not be trampled by winter boots. Had we not returned, and brought the dull season with us, Grundvik would have remained untouched by the chill that will now always remain.

There was nothing of the long days and warm nights we knew from our summers. I didn't venture out on Thursday mornings to wait for the mail boat. At night the water would freeze in the pipes.

I asked my dad one morning, when I couldn't turn on the tap: 'Where does all the water go?'

Dad smiled. 'It's still there, just frozen. Honey, ice is just frozen water, isn't it?' He laughed and pulled me to him.

When I walked out that morning I looked around at the heavy snow that covered everything and thought: it is all just water. But light and dazzling, and nothing like the black waves that surrounded the island.

My dad told us, while sitting by the fire one evening, that the ocean would be so cold now you would die within minutes if you fell in. It seemed as if the sea we had believed to be our tranquil friend, our comfort, had turned feral.

But we didn't really mind the cold. We were happy to be together and miss a couple of days of school. Helena and Toma were my best friends, and I had no reason to think anything would ever change.

The house on Grundvik Island belonged to Helena's parents. The island itself was public. Sometimes during the busy summer season boats would pull in and our beach would host strangers, but mostly we had it to ourselves. Helena's parents had opened a restaurant when they'd arrived in Sweden years before, and now Helena and her older brother went to expensive schools and on holidays to California. They didn't live in a high-rise; they had their own house with a large garden.

In Romania, Adrian, Toma's dad, had been a lawyer. When he came to Sweden he had been nothing for a long time before starting work as an office junior for an insurance firm.

He had big expectations of Toma, but Toma didn't have big ambitions. Toma wanted to watch movies and read comic books. He wanted to make friends and wander around town aimlessly with them.

Instead, he did three hours of homework on weekdays, five hours on the weekends, and took extra lessons in maths and German three times a week. The rest of his time Toma spent in his room – scared to disappoint, scared of the Chilean boys that lived on his block and scared of the names the Swedish kids called him at school.

During our summers on the island we would spend all of our time outside, either on the beach or in the forest. We sometimes even dared to go north to the cliffs, where we were forbidden to venture, and we would lay on our tummies right on the edge and watch the waves break, imagining what would happen if we fell.

But on our last visit, the winter visit, it got dark too early and was too cold to stay out late. So we hurried inside where there was, as always, food waiting, and picked an empty room to sit in, by a bright fire. Toma was even quieter than usual, and when he spoke he said things that made Helena and I look at each other with furrowed brows.

**

On the day of grandfather's party, Helena and I were outside after breakfast, eager to take advantage of the short day. Toma had been led by his father to the small office at the back of the house and instructed to translate a news article from Swedish to German and from German to Romanian. During the summers Toma would get away with only an hour's work, but now, in the middle of term, he had to follow his normal routine.

Helena and I snuck around the house and knocked on the window of his prison. Toma looked up at us with a little smile, then back down at his notes.

We pressed cold faces and mittened paws against the glass until he got up from the desk and opened the window.

'Poor Toma.'

'We've been on the cliff.'

'We've seen bits of a shipwreck. We'll show it to you. It's right under our place: a real shipwreck.'

'What's "shipwreck" in German, Toma?'

We sniggered as he leaned out of the window, snatched my fluffy hat and put it on his own head.

Suddenly, the door swung open. Helena and I ducked below the windowsill, covering our mouths in an attempt to stifle the giggles. Toma's dad slammed the window shut, glass rattling above us, his voice a low murmur. We couldn't make out his words, but they were followed by the sound of impact; something fell off the desk with a rustle, and then a second heavy thump.

Our hands still covered our mouths, but above the brightly coloured mittens our eyes weren't laughing anymore. The door was opened and slammed shut again, and we lifted our heads just enough to glance into the room, where Toma was at the desk again, his shoulders shaking and his face turned away from us.

I wanted to knock on the window again, but Helena took my hand and tugged gently and we ran off and hid among the skeletons of the oak and maple trees, where my mum found us a while later. She handed me back my hat and pulled me into a long embrace, and I could see, even then, that she knew it wasn't fair.

A few hours later, we were collecting stones on the beach when, through the quickly rising darkness, we saw Toma making his way down from the house.

He didn't look at us, just sat down, and we joined him in silence on the wet granite.

The sea was nothing but sparks in the dark.

'I hate German.'

'Yeah ...'

'I hate him.'

There was no need to ask who *he* was. His mark had been left on Toma's cheek and was visible even in the premature darkness of the winter afternoon. We said nothing, but Helena put her hand on Toma's arm.

Toma stood up and looked down at us, his face in shadows. 'I have an idea, come on.'

We followed him down to the pier and up to the boat that lay rocking. He jumped in.

'Toma! We're not allowed.'

'We have to get back for the party ...'

'You scared?'

Yes, we were, and we couldn't understand why he wasn't: his dad would be furious, but we jumped in next to him and looked at each other, trying to find encouragement.

Toma untied the knot that held boat and pier together, that held everything together, and pushed out with one of the oars.

We were alone in the inky night, drifting further and further from the lights of the house and the shrinking island. Helena was holding my hand and Toma was rowing with his back to us, his shoulders moving back and forth rhythmically and his breath rising above his head in puffs.

The cold filled my lungs as I drew breath after breath of salty air, and soon the comforting lights of our house were so distant they might have been just stars in the night.

When we stopped, we were in between Grundvik and the three small islands to the north. They were uninhabited and, now, only slightly blacker bumps in the black before us. Toma stood up, the boat swinging wildly, and Helena squeezed my hand.

'Toma, sit down!'

My father had told us, when he had found us huddled on the beach the previous evening, that the sea was as deep as the distance from Grundvik to the mainland. He had sat down next to us and I had squeezed myself into his warm side, feeling so safe with his arm around me, so warm, that nothing seemed further than the bottom of the sea.

Now, as drops of ice splashed up and burned my cheek, I found myself whispering 'daddy, daddy', desperately trying not to cry.

The oars dropped over the sides and with dull splashes sank to the bottom of the night.

When Toma turned around, the boat rocking unsteadily below us, we saw that he was crying. We couldn't see the tears, but his face was twisted and he kept wiping at it in angry jerks that shook the boat and made us squeal.

'Toma! Toma! Please sit down, please!'

Helena was also crying, and squeezing my hand so hard it made me wince.

'I'm not going back.'

'Don't be an idiot, Toma, we have to go back! We're going home tomorrow. Why did you drop the oars?'

Toma raised his chin and looked up at the sky above us,

a black spread to match the black of the sea below, both vast and deep and hungry.

'I'm not going back,' he said again, looking down.

I tried to catch his eye. There was something in his voice that scared me and I thought I could understand it better if I could just see his eyes. Helena knew more, she had dropped to her knees and was trying to pull him down, she was saying 'don't, Toma, don't' and I wasn't sure what he shouldn't.

And then the boat rocked and Toma leaned back, and for a moment he seemed to be leaning on the night.

We would never say anything other than that he had lost his balance.

The exact spot where it had happened remained unknown. There was no chasm in the sea where he had fallen and the body was never found.

There were no more visits to Grundvik Island. We left the house, just abandoned it. We left the beach and the cliffs. We left the pier to rot away.

We left the unbroken surface of the Baltic, and beneath it we left one of us.

Love

One night when I was ten years old, I found my mum crying in the kitchen.

I had awoken in the middle of the night, unsure of what had pulled me out of a bonbon dream that was instantly forgotten. I crept out of bed and opened the door of my room, gazing suspiciously up and down the hall beyond. All the lights in the house were off, and the first thing to pinch me through the darkness was the smell of cigarette smoke.

It was a smell I instantly associated with early mornings and coffee, with the pre-school rush and Radio 4, and it seemed out of place slinking down the corridors in the middle of the night. So I followed it to the kitchen, where I found her perched on the single barstool, guiding the orange ember of a cigarette.

Smoke curled around her silhouette and stung my eyes, and even before I could see the look on her face, or hear the quiver in her voice, I knew something was wrong. I knew with the instinctive knowledge of a creature under threat. I knew with the sudden unease in my stomach, with the sudden desire to run away.

When she spoke, her voice was soft and calm, and only the most sensitive of ears could have perceived the danger.

'Daddy doesn't love me anymore,' she said to me, with that shattering voice.

'Who does he love?' I asked, for a moment believing it was a game, a riddle.

I had stopped in the doorway, a couple of metres away from where she sat, and now my mother reached out to me, her arm white and ghostly through the night. The gold bracelet on her wrist, the bracelet she never removed, gleamed once then fell into darkness.

I took a step towards her, then another, and let myself be pulled into her arms, where she held me for a long while, her cigarette too close to my cheek and her breath stirring the hairs on the back of my neck.

Love was a foreign object then. It was like a strange instrument, beautiful and tempting in its intricate construction, but of unknown purpose, mysterious function. It was the reason for so many things and the explanation that never made sense. Love earned pretty declarations in rhyme from one, and suicide bids on dirty napkins from another. It was at times puritanical and hostile, as in the lofty promises of Hollywood films, and at times dark and haunting, like in the lyrics of Leonard Cohen, or in certain poems that explained so little but wafted a crisp, luscious feeling.

I had, at the tender age of ten, the inkling that what I had witnessed the previous summer, back in Romania, had been in part legitimate love and in part illegitimate.

My auntie Cristina and her fiancé had stood holding hands before the priest and the congregation. Her mother had cried openly, the adults had danced all evening and into the next day, and I had experienced the drama of my first wedding, grasping the significance of the event in the same academic way that I knew the world to be large and Pluto to be far away.

The whole family had come together, from as far away as

Canada, and gathered in the picturesque mountain village that boasted a painted monastery, to witness the union between Cristina and Jack.

My parents and I knew Jack from London, and he had been introduced to Cristina at a barbecue the previous year when she had come to spend a summer with us, her London relatives. After their first meeting, Jack visited us every day. He received heavy encouragement from my mother, who knew enough about him to consider him quality husband material: he had a job, a university education and wanted children.

Cristina was twenty-seven and, though quite beautiful in a sultry, emaciated kind of way, was considered to be playing her last hand in the game of love and marriage.

Cristina did not speak a single word of English, and as my mother and father supposedly had better things to do, it fell onto me to play translator.

For a good ten days I ran back and forth between the amorous couple and one or another of my parents, asking how to say this in English, or what that meant in Romanian. On one occasion, my mother sent me back to Jack translationless but with the suggestion that he subdue his enthusiasm a tad.

Mum got Jack a Romanian language course on tape, and before Cristina went back home he naively forced me, the annoyed nine-year-old, to teach him how to say 'It has been a pleasure to meet you and I hope to see you again soon' in Romanian.

At Heathrow, after the twelve-day romance, Jack informed us all that he would be visiting Cristina in Romania the following month, and that his intentions were of the most serious nature. They kissed, passionately, and my mother welled up and squeezed my hand.

For one moment Cristina's black, black eyes flickered to my father, like a dying light, and he looked away at the planes taking off on the runway outside the walls of glass.

As Cristina, looking fresh and happy in spite of the tears, made her way towards the passport check, Jack rushed forward in a passion that made the security guards jump, and yelled that he will be her waiter tonight and the evening's specialty was the pan-fried liver.

Exactly a year later we received the wedding invitations.

It was the first time we had visited Romania since our exodus in the early eighties, and I had no memory of the place. When we finally arrived in the village where the wedding was to take place, hot and exhausted after a long day's travel, I was attacked by an onslaught of perky and entirely unknown aunties, uncles and cousins who all claimed to have known me when I was tiny.

Those couple of days before the wedding, when all the grown-ups had been busy, were magic. I made best friends instantly. I had never known such freedom. In our cramped little terrace house in north-west London I had never felt the joy of mountains and fields and wilderness.

After the wedding ceremony I had gone, by myself, to lie in the field, look up at an enormous sky and wish things could be like this forever.

That's where I was when I saw my father and my auntie Cristina walking on the border of the wooded land that extended to the west, towards Doina. There had been nothing strange about their behaviour, nor about their presence. They were walking, simply walking; my father in his dark suit and Cristina in the white dress that looked fluorescent in the dimming light, and which the wind licked around her body, so she was forced to hold it down with her hands. Her hair was up and her shoulders bare and my father cupped one of his large hands over a milky shoulder, swallowing it whole.

They stopped on the border of the forest, right on the edge, giant oak and maple reaching with lush branches, reaching down towards them, wanting to pull them into the gloom, into the wilderness.

He was smiling. His big childish face stretched wide in a joy I had until that moment thought belonged only to me and, before any other wisdom, there came the sharp twinge of jealously, quickly followed by something else.

It came, as my father's smile fell, and his face darkened as if the shadows of those trees had left the forest and were advancing across the field.

Another emotion, like fear; like losing control of your bike down a steep hill or losing sight of your mother in a crowded supermarket. But this was the fear of losing something else, something so huge that it couldn't be seen.

My father was, to me, my world. He made the rain fall and the sun shine, and I knew completely and with unwavering certainty that I was his world, and until this moment I had never believed it possible that things could be any other way.

In that field, on that evening, nothing made sense – not my father's white knuckles as he dug his fingers into Cristina's flesh, not Cristina's grimace at his grip, which might have been one of pain had she pulled away, but she did not pull away, and he dug in and clawed his way across her back, beneath the low cut of her glowing dress.

I jumped up and ran towards them, leaving my shoes

behind. It was in the moment that my father turned to me, the moment his eye fell on me, that I felt the affirmation of something forbidden, as if I had eavesdropped on a secret conversation.

For one instant, my father looked a stranger to me, and looked at me like a stranger, like he had been looking at Cristina before he could rearrange his face. Everything warm and comforting seemed in that moment vanished, and instead I felt a threat, harsh, urgent, and I stopped dead, like prey in the glare of the lion.

And then he was back, himself again, asking me where I had been rolling around, and warning me of my mother's predictable displeasure at the grass stains on my stockings and the twigs in my hair.

At that moment I longed to be back in England, back in Kilburn, where things were of cement and made sense.

That night, with my mother in the kitchen, I had the feeling that love was a thing you can equally give away or withdraw; like a gift, bestow upon someone or snatch back. But that when it is drawn back it continues to take and take of you, like the never-ending chain of bright handkerchiefs that the magician pulls from his pocket.

After that short, mysterious exchange in the dark, my mother roused herself out of her melancholy, looking at me with infinite tenderness, and asked what I was doing up at that time. She took me by the hand to my room and tucked me into bed, caressing my hair and warning me that there would be no excuses for not getting up for school the next day.

At that moment I thought I wanted the truth. I thought that the truth was love and I felt wounded by my mother's silence.

I couldn't have known that love was swallowing that

bitter truth and allowing me to grow up, soon forgetting about the incident, happy and protected, with the heroes of my little world intact, safe in the knowledge that whatever love was, it lived, unchallenged and unthreatened, with me.

Returned

It had been two days before they'd found the old man, so Magge Ericksson tells me.

On midsummer's eve all the young girls had run off to the fields and to the woods to pluck flowers, and his little Ulla had joined them.

'Marie's daughter,' he says, 'you remember my Marie? You remember kissing her?'

I remembered. Magge points with his cane towards the copse of oak and elder that has always surrounded the house. With every gust, these guardians sigh deeply, their crowns rippling like green foam.

'You remember hiding in those woods?' Magge chuckles and wipes his mouth with a clean white handkerchief.

'You were frightened then, isn't that so? So frightened you climbed the tallest tree and wouldn't come down again. Such a wet lad ... but all the girls liked you well enough, didn't they?'

He gives a toothless grin and lays a large, rough hand on my shoulder.

'She was my first love, Marie,' I say, smiling at the memory of happiness that even then seemed impossible, evanescent, like the sweetest thing ever so briefly ripened before spoiling.

'She has three little girls of her own,' Magge says. 'Ulla is the youngest, and just like her mother; you can't keep her still, you can't keep her quiet. Like quicksilver, that lass. They've all moved to the city, of course, like all the young people in this place. But the little one likes to come and visit.'

We stand in silence, Magge and I, and it is a fond,

comfortable lull. The sun has dropped to its lowest point and the woods, the fields, the houses on the slope beyond, lean against the stark grey light.

Every night, all summer long, the sun in this place skims the horizon, threatening with a perpetual dusk that never settles into darkness.

I had forgotten. I had forgotten covering the windows of my bedroom with old blankets, desperate for the dark, for a moment's peace. I had forgotten that half-light; insidious, playing softly on the floorboards, through the cracks, between the blinds.

On my first night back, kept awake by the murmur of light, I remembered. I walked through the house, restless, hearing whispers, creaks; the house a living thing with me in its belly, the walls like skin, too thin to block out the dull glare of a dogged sun.

I opened doors and watched dust stir and settle. The old office smelled of damp. Maps were spread open on the desk, faded by time, and a fountain pen lay poised against a crystal inkwell, encrusted with dry ink and as opaque as granite in the twilight. The wooden floorboards, bare and uneven, bore testimony of restless nights spent pacing to and fro between the bookshelves and the locked glass-fronted cabinet. How many nights had he spent guarding his treasures, I wondered. How many vigils had been held against the dark, against the hordes of thieves and gypsies that would come to loot and destroy, if only they would come.

My sisters' old room, with the twin beds side by side and the collection of dolls, was as it had always been, like it would always be: a tribute to purity, a pretty pink lie. The bookshelf in the corner of the room held no books, but cheap trinkets and porcelain angels with perfect hands, frozen wings, faces full of blank submission. This was a little girls' room, but the little girls who had lived there were young women, their betrayal as natural as it was abhorrent.

Half-light breathed half-life into the past, and for a moment I thought I saw the milky faces of twenty-three angels turn on me: twenty-three pairs of dead eyes demanding an explanation.

I slammed the door shut.

***

He was dead. He was gone. I had flown in from London on the day I'd received the news to make sure. Elina, the elder of my sisters, had called through to the office, demanding that I be pulled out of my meeting to speak with her.

'He's dead,' she'd said.

'He's ...'

'Dead. Old Magge found him.'

'How?'

'They think he fell down the stairs, cracked his head open. Like an egg.'

I turned away from the glass wall that separated my office from the main floor. 'Lina, are ... you going down there? Is Annika?'

'She can't. Annika can't. And I've got the kids this week ... Albert?'

'I know. I'll get there as soon as I can, tonight if I can get on a flight.'

I arrived late in the evening at Arlanda, and picked up the hired family saloon, the only car available, to drive the 250-odd kilometres north-west. In spite of all the years, I had no difficulty finding the way, and stopped only once to fill up the car and get enough supplies to last a couple of days.

A few hours later, I turned off the main road, heading up towards the three lakes that were Lilla, Mellan and Stora Justasjöarna. Every field, every barn, every turn in the road seemed familiar to me; so much so that I had the feeling I could have closed my eyes and navigated by instinct alone.

The largest of the lakes lay in the first valley and as I crested the peak I saw its wide, tranquil face, holding a perfect expression of the sky, the hills, the weeping willows that fringed its shores. A raptor soared above, and then dipped low, leaving, but for a moment, a scar in its wake.

I found the narrow track that ran along the western side of the lake, through the woods, and followed it, higher and higher.

When the car could go no further on the rough track, I left it in a ditch and walked the rest of the way.

***

I was awake all night, walking up and down stairs and corridors, standing on thresholds, and finally lying on the floor of the living room where I had made my bed. I'm not sure when I finally fell asleep, but by the time I stirred awake the sun was low on the horizon.

I got dressed and walked out, through the woods and down to the fence, where I found Magge, waiting as if he'd known to expect me. I offered him my left hand to shake, keeping my right behind my back, as, though I have nothing to hide from Magge, is my habit.

'She came back with seven flowers and put them under

her pillow, like all the girls do, and do you know what the child dreamt of, Albert?' Magge says.

'Not of her future husband, then?'

'Not that.'

'They never do. My sisters never did.'

Magge watches me calmly beneath bushy eyebrows, as white and wiry as his hair.

'Your sisters are here?'

'No, just me.'

'Nice girls, your sisters. Are they married now?'

'Elina was. Annika has a boyfriend, I think.'

'They never did come back, did they? A better life in the city, I suppose. An easy life.'

'Better, perhaps.'

'And you went even further, Albert? You never came back either.'

'I didn't have much to come back to,' I say.

Magge looks up, towards the house, his eyes following the memory of what had been a path, leading from the gate through the trees and up to the front yard. Now, instead of woodchips and gravel, moss is soft underfoot, long grass and gnarly roots having reclaimed the trail, order having given way to the gentle, inexorable chaos of nature.

'She dreamt of your old man,' Magge says, watching me.

'Marie's girl did?'

'And the next day I come to check on him, and find him dead as anything, with his head opened on the flagstones.'

'Where did they take him?'

'Lundberg came for the body.'

'Thank you,' I say.

'We could have done more for you ... for you and for your

sisters. It's too late now, but we could have done more.'

Magge takes one final survey of the place, his eyes skidding on me as he turns and makes his slow, laboured way back down the hill, to the shore of the smallest lake and his own comfortable home, lonely now perhaps, silent with the absence of children and grandchildren, but full of happy warm memories and one ugly grain of guilt.

***

We used to swim in Lilla Justa every year, as early as April. As soon as the snow melted in the ditches and the days outgrew the nights, we'd anticipate the weekend when he'd be called to town. We'd wait for the diesel rumble from the back of the house where the forest had been cleared into a gravelled yard, which narrowed into a track that curled around the hills and into town. We'd listen until the rattle ebbed, until it was a hum, and finally just a suspicion drowned out by the twittering of birds and rush of the lively spring breeze. Only then would I tiptoe to my sisters' room, barefoot and holding my breath against the fumes of exhaust that always lingered. Elina would be ready, wearing her swimsuit beneath jeans and a woolly jumper.

'He's gone,' I'd report, and Elina's face would brighten in anticipation. She'd snatch the blanket from our little sister's bed and tug her out.

'Come, Annika, get ready. We have to go.'

Annika would let Elina pull the nightgown over her head. She'd step obediently into the faded pink swimsuit, and then into the jeans and sweater, while weeping all along.

'But what if he comes back?' she'd say, her voice soft and trembling, as Elina tied her long golden hair into a braid.

'But what if he comes back?' she'd say, looking

desperately from one to the other, as Elina and I took her by the hands and led her outside.

And we would gather – my sisters and I, Marie and her brothers, and a few younger kids – by the shore, to see who was brave enough to take the first swim. A wooden jetty poked out into the middle of the lake and we'd jostle each other to the very end, our toes over the edge, holding back until the first of us jumped and then we all joined in, shrieking, laughing, in the icy water.

Magge and his wife, Marie's parents, watched us from the vantage point of the granite outcrop that joined their backyard to the lake. They waited with blankets and hot chocolate for us to race back to the house, half-frozen and shivering but happy.

Later, we walked back home, Elina, Annika, and I, still laughing and teasing until we turned the corner and saw the little wood, our wood, swaying before us. And we slowed, our limbs like lead, and walked in silence until we reached the gate. Annika would cry, and sometimes I did too though I tried not to.

'We shouldn't have gone,' Annika sobbed, 'we should have been good.'

'We said we would. We all said it, Anni.'

'Yes, but it was wrong, we ...'

'It wasn't wrong. We always go for the first swim together.'

Elina took our sister's hand as we crept along the path.

'Anni, don't be afraid. It will be bad for a little bit but then it will be okay. You had a nice time, didn't you? It was lovely, wasn't it?'

'We should have been good ...'

I open the front door and step inside. Our grandfather built the house on the site of an old farmyard, preserving what had once been the flagstones of an inner court in our hall and kitchen. This stone floor is always cold, always damp, and now, at the foot of the stairs that lead to the first floor, it is stained brown with my father's blood.

I had looked away from it when I'd first arrived, but now I stand with my toes on the edge of the very last blood the old man will ever spill. I feel a chill rising from the stones, through my flesh, through by bones, and I try to warm myself up with thoughts of hell.

I never fully believed in either heaven or hell as a child. I wondered then why, if there was such a thing as a God who had created the world and all its beasts, he would hate my sisters for growing out of their childhood forms.

Elina was the first to disappoint. She had received her eleventh, and final, angel, and woken up the next day to find herself stained with womanhood. The eleven angels on their shelf could offer no explanation, no comfort.

'So now you are a whore, like Eve, like your mother,' he'd said, and punished us all for it.

Later Annika asked her sister why she'd done it.

'Why couldn't you be good? That's all father wants, that we be good so we can be angels in heaven.'

I don't know how long I have been here. I know it's been a day at least, and I have yet to deal with any of the things I have come here for. I have not contacted the undertaker, or the lawyer. Nobody at St Gabriel's has been asked to dig a hole.

I am sitting on a rug, eating the last of my provisions, when my mobile cuts into the silence.

'How is it?' Elina asks.

I can hear her kids laughing in the background, and suddenly I think that I might cry.

'Albert? Are you there?'

'I am.'

'How is it?'

'If you cared, you could have come yourself. You or Annika could have come.'

'What? Albert, what ...'

'I say let's forget about this. I don't need the money. Do you? Do you think Annika wants his money? I say let's leave it as it is. Fuck it. Burn it down. It doesn't matter to me.'

Elina's breath is jagged and quick; she's somewhere else now, in another room, and I can't hear the kids anymore.

'Okay, Albert. That's okay with me.'

***

The silence is absolute and cannot be concealed by wind or birdsong. I lay listening to my own heartbeat and hoping that sleep will come.

I open my eyes and see his face for the briefest of moments. It is the face I last saw fifteen years ago. It is a smooth, noble face, with clear blue eyes and a thin mouth.

He opens his mouth and I wake up screaming, covered in sweat.

I get dressed and spend a while going through the stack of documents, bills, letters, that he kept locked in his desk. I wasn't able to find the key and had to use a screwdriver to break open the drawers, shattering wood and making a mess of splinters, the fine dust getting into my throat and refusing to settle. Why he wished to keep this junk under lock and key is a mystery; I find no scandalous correspondence, no revelations – just four decades of household bills and contracts.

I hear a sound outside, like tiny bells, and go to the window. It is a bright, warm day and, among the long grass and ancient trees, I spot something small and nimble.

Outside, I walk a few steps into the shade of the thicket and wait. There is a rustle, and something peeks out from behind a huge old oak. Older than the house, older than whatever homestead was here before the house, its branches hang low, like the arms of a giant, and its trunk is as wide as a shed around the base.

The little girl steps out and watches me as I watch her. She smiles, and I feel something warm and familiar spread through me.

'Hello, Ulla,' I say.

She frowns and takes a step closer.

'I don't know you,' she says.

'My name is Albert.'

'Oh well, I know that. I know your name is Albert and you used to kiss my mum. And you don't have a hand.'

I lift my right hand and wiggle my two remaining fingers.

'See, I do,' I say.

'That's not a hand. That's just two fingers. You're supposed to have...' she frowns, considering, 'you're supposed to have five. Five fingers.'

She's wearing a white summer dress with bare feet, and old Magge was right, she is the spitting image of her mother.

She was a beautiful, kind child.

Marie.

She was never what you expected her to be. When we were little, she was wise and patient. She waited for the smaller kids to catch up, and never teased them for being slow through the wood or scared of the dark. When we were older, while the rest of us stumbled through as awkward adolescents, she glided through a world of old toys abandoned for new yearnings without fear or hesitation. When someone, a stranger or a neighbour, would note how pretty she was, how extraordinarily fair and sweet, Marie would laugh and say that everything around here was beautiful and sweet.

Every winter, on the thirteenth of December, Marie was our Lucia. She would tour the village dressed in a white gown, a red ribbon around her waist, a crown of candles on her head and a train of little girls in white following behind. They would give out warm *lussebullar* to the crowd that always gathered, and they would sing songs and walk through the snow from St Gabriel's to the school, holding candles against the winter darkness.

During the short walk outside, parents would run around the train of kids, bundling them up in coats and pulling on woolly hats, offering mittens and hot chocolate from thermoses. They'd rush ahead to the school and wait by the front doors to pull off coats and hats.

One day Marie was waiting for me after class. It was a long walk around Mellan Justa, through the village that huddled by its shore, and back up the hill to our houses. Some of the kids rode their bicycles, but I didn't have one and enjoyed the distance.

Marie was waiting by the edge of the playground, where it dipped into a narrow field. A path ran through the grassland, now covered in snow, and we stepped out together, our boots crunching on the gravel. Later in the winter the lake would freeze solid, and we'd be able to cut across it, straight to the tiny crescent beach behind the post office, but for now only a thin crust of ice lay gleaming on its surface. The deep snow muffled sounds, hushing the world and filling the early dark with sparks.

Marie took my hand. She was bundled up in a heavy coat, hat and scarves, only her eyes and the pink of her cheeks showing. I felt her fingers, hard and determined, through her mitten, and thought that she must feel mine, limp and uncertain, through my thin glove.

We didn't speak. We walked through the woods, beneath the bare branches of elms that scratched at the sky and beneath the dense pines and spruces that dropped loads of snow with heavy thuds.

And all the time she held my hand, and as we walked my fingers grew bolder, stronger, returning her grip with their own. I pulled off my glove and stuffed it in my pocket, and gently pulled off her mitten and let it dangle by its knitted cord. Her hand was warm and soft, and she did not complain about the cold. When we got to the crossroad where we would have to part, Marie took my hand to her mouth and touched her lips to it.

'You could kiss me, if you'd like to,' she whispered in my palm, her breath small white clouds.

I kissed Marie. We walked over the frozen ground and into the woods. In the dark, in the cold, I kissed Marie, and kissed her again, until I heard a snap and looked up to see one of Marie's little brothers watching us.

'Albert is kissing Marie,' he said, softly, and then louder, 'Albert and Marie are kissing, they are, they are!'

He grinned at us, and set off at a run down the hill, awkward in his padded overalls, slipping and falling and getting up again.

It took a day for my father to find out. We were out chopping wood in the twilight, my father and I, when Magge came strolling down the path from our house.

'I've got your generator in my truck,' Magge said, watching us work with knuckles on hips. 'Icy as hell; I don't know how I'll make it back down the hill again. I may end up helping you bring down a few trees.'

My father handed me the axe and shook Magge's hand. He asked if Magge would like some coffee, back at ours.

'Thank you, but I should get back. How are you, Albert? Cold, isn't it, son?'

I could tell, from his smile, from the twinkle in his eye; I could tell what was coming. I put down the axe and began to back away, stumbling on a knot of roots and landing flat on my back.

'Take it easy, boy,' Magge laughed, 'she was going to get kissed sooner or later, and I much prefer you to that loud-mouthed Axelson kid.'

I ran. I ran through the woods and found the tallest tree, and I took off my gloves and jacket and scurried up the branches like a squirrel. I could hear Magge laughing and chatting, telling my father what had happened, telling him how sweetly Marie must have blushed, and how lovely it is to be young and foolish and in love.

A while later I heard Magge's truck splutter and wheeze; I heard it skid down the track, the brakes squealing.

And then I heard heavy footsteps through the snow, and my father's face emerged beneath me, between the branches.

'I'll wait here all night, boy. I'll wait until you fall down,' he said, the axe balanced on his shoulder, the steel white with the moon.

And he did.

***

'What's wrong?' Ulla asks, a frown between her pale eyebrows.

She has come closer still, and is balancing on a granite boulder, arms out, hopping on one leg and then the other.

I feel, as I sometimes do when it is cold, the phantom

sensation of my missing fingers. I feel them as I clutch my hand into a fist.

'He is upset, you know,' Ulla says, and jumps down from the rock, taking a seat on it instead.

Her cheeks are chubby like all little pups, and she has two front teeth missing. She's watching me, her eyes focused and unblinking, and jiggles with her thumb what's soon going to be another missing tooth.

'Who is upset?' I ask.

'Your dad. He is very sorry, he said.'

I stare at the girl. 'What are you saying? When did you speak to him?'

'In my dream. He was very upset. Mister? What's in the black box behind the glass?'

'I don't...'

'He said that there is something in the black box behind the glass. He is upset, your daddy. He is dead, isn't he?'

I struggle to remain standing, and I think that, if I can get inside the house, I might be able to sleep. Finally, I might be able to get some rest, and then tomorrow I will leave. There is nothing I can do here. I'll phone the lawyer from the road and ask him to get rid of the house: sell it, burn it, give it away, whatever he wants. I'll send Lundberg a cheque and tell him to do with the body what he usually does with unwanted, unclaimed remains.

'Go home, Ulla. Go play somewhere else.'

'But...'

'Leave!'

It comes out harsher than I mean it to and the child blinks at me a few times before getting to her feet and running off, her steps almost silent on the thick, soft moss.

'He is right,' she shouts over her shoulder, 'you *are* bad!'

Inside, it is cold and dank, so I light a fire and begin

to stuff my things back into my bag. I want to be ready to go, first thing in the morning. I don't want to think before then. I want to lie down and slip into nothing, dream of nothing, feel nothing.

I switch off my mobile and close my eyes, my right hand still tingling.

He comes to me as well. I am looking at him from above, from between branches, as I did that one day, long ago. I want to wake up, but it's a long way down and the branch I'm holding onto is slippery and wet.

My father's watching me. His face is clear and the night is bright with the moonlight and the snow.

You bleed like a pig, he says, and his lips don't move. I'll wait here all night. I'll wait until you fall down.

And with a scream I do fall down, through the branches, and land in the snow whipped and torn.

I struggle to get to my feet, tangled up in blankets and half-asleep.

The fire has gone out and it is very cold. I look out through a window and am surprised to find that it is still summer outside.

I grab my bag, hoping that the rental is still in the ditch where I left it. My mobile won't come back on, and I don't know what time it is, but I am sure I'll find a hotel along the way, and if not I'll drive all the way to Arlanda.

At the front door I stop and turn around.

I run up the stairs and into my father's office, stepping back into the mess of broken wood and old papers. I pick up the inkwell from the desk and hurl it at the cabinet, at my father's treasure chest.

I start back and swallow a cry when I see him again, young this time but wild, reflected in the glass the moment before it shatters.

I pick up objects – valuable, delicate objects, scientific instruments, things with dials and coils – and smash them into oblivion.

These were the things my father loved. He collected them to remind himself of the goodness in man. Of the great things, the great beauty, that man can achieve when he allows his soul to lead him.

When there is nothing left, I notice my hands are bleeding. I also notice, tucked away at the back, a small box.

The lid is stiff and I struggle to prise it open. I fumble and scratch, smudge it with blood, until it gives.

Inside are three small, dried twigs. I pick one up and take a closer look.

I shall be returning home a whole man, I think, putting my little finger back in the box.

The Impressionist

Worst of them all are the ones who really try, only to fail: the ones desperately seeking approval. Don't get me wrong, they are all desperate to please, perhaps we all are, but most balance this natural predisposition with the equally natural urge to rebel. In their case, rebellion manifests itself as a hearty commitment to ignorance.

Some days are a battle waged, but I don't believe that the real war is between teachers and students, only between hope and those things that break it. Those accumulated disappointments, the inevitable realisation that gravity always wins and what was once the soaring dream of *making a difference* comes crashing down, broken and scorched, as *just making it through the day*. We, the teachers, soon come to understand that we will not change young lives, and that the sword of knowledge we brandish so proudly might as well be a cheap lightsaber from Toys-R-Us. In turn, our young students eventually realise that their lives will never change, and that their vow to idiocy will ultimately remain unchallenged.

Some of them are, in fact, just idiots. It isn't their fault. I blame the absolute collapse of the structures, both private and public, that should provide a system for bringing up well-balanced, educated adults. These kids will not grow up well-balanced or educated; I've met many of their parents. Most of these kids have been handed a genetic dud by Mother Nature and my classroom is just a pit stop on the way to nowhere.

Then there are some – namely, Helen Lowie of 8a – who try to win brownie points by reading ahead of the class and handing in work I have not asked for. Helen

Lowie once handed in a twelve-page poem, 308 lines, all in rhyme.

'What did you think, Miss Lessing?' she asked me a week later.

'It was ... very interesting, Helen,' I lied, not having the heart to tell her that life is too short for bad poetry, and that my life in particular, the life of a teacher, is so prosaic that the very idea of 154 rhymes sets me into a cold panic.

Mr Tomaki, maths and physics teacher at Bowlinton Academy, has calculated that seventeen per cent of female students will have a baby before graduation. He also calculated that eighty-six per cent of the teachers will have experienced violence in the classroom within their first year, and that, statistically, we are safer on a Monday than on a Thursday.

I get on well with Mr Tomaki.

When Mr Tomaki was stabbed in the leg a few years back, I visited him at the hospital every afternoon. After a few shots of cheap vodka, Mr Tomaki confessed to me that the second before Marc Tyles, 6b, took the blade out of his shoe and stuck it into his teacher's thigh, Mr Tomaki had been about to punch the boy straight in the face. Mr Tomaki concluded that, all in all, being stabbed had saved his career and spared him a life sentence in jail for bashing in a child's head while screaming 'per cent *is* out of one hundred, per cent is *always* out of one hundred!'

The incident got some media attention, and for a few

days journalists would appear in the schoolyard asking for comments. Though most of the comments were unprintable, they did manage to get an interview with Mrs Dexter, our Head, and Helen Lowie, 8a. Mrs Dexter, coiffed and wearing the suit she usually reserves for parents' evening, told the *Standard* that she was taking the incident very seriously and that such behaviour was not to be tolerated.

Helen Lowie told the reporter that everyone carried knives, and that they had stopped the after-school club, which was a shame as it had been good fun, and kids enjoyed playing table tennis and other stuff.

The *Evening Standard* printed an article on how cuts to funding in education have led to violent crime, along with a photo of Mrs Dexter looking as if she's trying to sell something.

Helen Lowie was asked never to speak to a journalist again. So, instead, she wrote another poem and this time asked me to read it while she was waiting. There she stood. Tall, skinny, pale in her maroon uniform, her jacket too big and her eyes full of need behind the NHS prescription glasses.

And I did, at that moment, allow myself to feel a twinge of pity for this girl who asked for so much. I wanted to tell her to stop wanting. I wanted to tell Helen that I knew she didn't have many friends and that her mother had unrealistic expectations, but that the approval she needed would not come from me. I wanted to take her little hand and say to her: 'Honey, give it up. Don't fight a losing battle. Look around you. Out of all these kids how many do you think will achieve anything real? Not even one per cent. Not even half of that. Some will end up in decent, menial jobs, most will go on the dole, or get pregnant by sixteen, fall down the rabbit hole. None will find wings to soar. All of the things you see on TV – the superstars, the platinum, the fame – that's all a lie. It is not real, at least not for you, so stop wanting to be special and get on with being yourself. It may not be much, but at least it's honest and real, and it will spare you disappointment.'

I wanted to tell her this because at that moment I forgot just how annoying Helen of 8a was, and I saw her as a little girl with high hopes, who probably still played with dolls and believed in happily-ever-afters.

I said none of these things but instead explained to Helen that I had a mountain of assessments to get through, which was true, and that I would read her poem later, which was not.

But Helen Lowie is the exception.

Most of them just sit at the back of the classroom and update their Facebook, message their friends. They watch music videos and read magazines and are obsessed with the unholy trinity of money, celebrity and sex. The boys talk about hitting the music scene and get into fights over what rapper is the hardest. I have seen an argument over Kanye West (is he a sellout or is he not?) escalate into a violent row between two packs of delinquents that lasted for weeks and involved three police call-outs.

The girls wear too much make-up and talk like everything they are is up for sale. They think the only way to get ahead is by being sexy and mean, and it is mostly the girls, not the boys, who use the word *dyke* behind my back, just loud enough for me to hear. They've nicknamed me Lessie the Lesbo, and their ringleader, Janeen Carlson, makes a show out of flirting with me after class. She'll lean over my desk, her plump, overly developed breasts nearly popping out of her shirt. She'll lick her lip gloss off her lips, and smile at me like the Big Bad Wolf.

Janeen is the kind of girl who wears size twelve though she's a sixteen, and who's constantly being told off by Mrs Dexter for rolling up her skirt. Janeen wears bright purple eye shadow and though she is not the prettiest girl in school, she's managed to accrue a number of disciples who follow her around like shadows, wear her shade of purple and get into fights on her behalf.

I remember when Janeen first started at Bowlinton, three years ago. She was a sweet little kid, who was teased because her mum did her hair, and not very well. In her second year, she was taken out mid-term and spirited off to Jamaica to attend her grandfather's funeral. Janeen returned to school with a new hairstyle and a brand new attitude; gone was the sweet little girl with the lopsided braids, her place taken up by a nubile young woman, too aware of her powers, and too eager to use them for evil.

After Janeen flaunts her cleavage, licks her lips, and smiles, she scurries off with her friends, all laughing like maniacs at how outrageous she is. If I cared enough, I would take Janeen aside and have a quiet chat with her. I would tell her that she doesn't have to please everyone and that being popular only means being like everyone else. I would ask Janeen what she has that's original; what could she offer the world? I'd ask her what her dream was, and no matter how stupid, I'd tell her she could make it happen.

One evening, while reading updates from a food journalist I admire, I come across a tweet from Colin Archer, 7b. A few years ago, in an moment of boredom and morbid curiosity, I set up a Twitter account under the name of Trojanee Orse. I followed a few of the ringleaders, including Colin. It provides good fodder for the book I'm not writing. This particular tweet read:

'Eng Lit wit Miss Lesbo... Or iz it Mista??? Holla back Dee!!!'

To which Derick Marshal, also of 7b, had replied:

'Id stil give it her bruv..... Make the biatch scream!!!!!'

I print this out and take it with me to my next session, where I ask the class to rewrite the two tweets into a language that might pass for something spoken by actual humans, preferably English.

After the initial shock wears off, the class sets to work and for the first time in the six months that I have had the pleasure of being ignored by 7b, the little bastards actually do what I ask them to, and though I am in fact an agnostic, I experience the urge to fall down to my knees and praise Jesus.

Derick and Colin look thoroughly concerned, worried that this will equal exclusion and that the rewriting of their abuse is just an elaborate entrapment meant to incriminate them even further. They cast suspicious glances at each other, until Charleen Travis starts giggling, which sets the rest of the class off.

'Something amusing?'

'No, Miss, but like ...'

'What is it, Charleen?'

'Well, like, you know, we can't write this ...'

'And why is that?'

'You know...'

'I have set you an assignment for this lesson and I expect you to complete it, unless you'd rather go to Mrs Dexter's office?'

And they set back to work.

Immediately after my class is finished, I'm summoned to Mrs Dexter's office myself. This is how it often goes with her. She knows things before they've barely had a chance to happen, and it is the belief of the general teaching staff that she's got informants among the students.

'What do you think you are doing, Miss Lessing?' Dexter demands the moment I crack open her door. She fixes me with her pale blue eyes; eyes that look like they belong in another face, a younger, more beautiful face.

'I don't know what you mean,' I lie.

'What just took place in your lesson, Miss Lessing?'

'Well, I thought ...'

'You should have brought the abusive emails to me. Immediately. You should not have brought them into class.'

'Tweets. They were abusive tweets. And I thought I'd try something a little different.'

'Must I remind you of the curriculum?'

When I first decided to qualify as a teacher, after spending eight years not writing my novel, I had a vision of changing lives. I replayed this private film in my head, starring me, *Dead Poets Society* meets *Dangerous Minds*, wisdom imparted, bonds made, young lives catapulted in new directions.

I had ideas, original ideas. Books I wanted to share, concepts to explore.

This was before I met The Curriculum.

And here I stand, face to face, with the Custodian of the National Curriculum. Mrs Laura Dexter, consummate bureaucrat, not even six months on the frontline. Not even six months. She knows nothing about standing before a pack of hungry dogs wearing your finest meat suit.

To Dexter it is all about passing OFSTED inspections and sweeping crap under the carpet. She only ever sees actual students when they are being punished. To her, teachers, students, classes, exams, are all equal figures that either add up, or do not.

And right now, I am not adding up.

Dexter doesn't know what to make of me. She's not comfortable with the whole alternative lifestyle thing, though she takes pride in having a real, live lesbian on her teaching staff. We don't have anything to talk about; she can't compliment me on my hairstyle or dress, and she's scared to ask what I did over the weekend.

Sometimes I look at her and see a politician, sometimes a magician. Right now I'm seeing Matron: stern, and displeased with my shenanigans.

I walk out of Dexter's office, suitably repentant, and say hello to her assistant, Marie.

'How's it going?' I ask.

'Great. And you?' she smiles.

Marie is always great, always smiling. She has two kids who look exactly like her, round and jolly.

Seated in one of the sofas is a girl I don't recognise. I look at Marie.

'Oh,' she says, 'Lea Olvi, this is Nina Lessing, she's our English teacher. Lea is Alice's new assistant.'

'Ah,' I say.

Alice, our lovely, terrified art teacher, has been crying for another classroom assistant since her last one left to become a yoga instructor. Alice is an actual working artist who hates teaching but is determined to martyr herself. In her own words: 'One must give back to society, however horrific it is.' I know that on three occasions she has completed students' final work herself, partly out of an unwillingness to officially call a kid a failure, and partly out of fear of the little failures and their mighty tempers.

Every evening Alice retreats to her studio in South Hampstead and produces evocative, modern sculptures that actually earn her a decent living. For the past five years, I have thought it only a question of time before Alice throws in the towel and gives up on the whole teaching thing, but though her career has gone from strength to strength, Alice continues her battle with apathy in Studio 2 of Bowlinton Academy.

She is the only one who ever asks about my novel, that great shining beacon on the horizon of my wasted opportunities.

I shake hands with Lea Olvi and ask when she's joining us. Lea looks young, maybe twenty-three, and has smooth, tanned skin. Her hair is very short, almost shaved. I ask if she's part Japanese.

'My mum's from Malaysia,' she says, flashing a smile, and then asks me to show her the tweets that have caused all the fuss.

I take out a printout and hand it to her while Marie retreats back to her desk, unwilling to be part of an activity that has been condemned by her commander-in-chief.

'Mate, what bastards. Did they rewrite it?'

'Yep.'

'I bet you they were pissing themselves,' Lea laughs.

The door to Dexter's office opens and she sticks her head out, watches us suspiciously for one moment and then decorates her face with her most winning smile.

'If you want to come through, Miss Olvi?' Dexter says, and Lea stands up to leave.

As she's entering Dexter's office she turns and smiles at me one last time, and I notice that in addition to perfect skin and great bone structure, the girl's also got dimples.

As the door closes, I see Marie watching me.

'She's very cute,' Marie says, with meaning.

'Like a button,' I agree and walk off, contemplating nipples.

***

I step into my classroom the following Monday to find Lea Olvi sitting on my desk, with her feet in my chair. She's wearing all white, a good choice, and turning the pages of my *Best American Short Stories*. She doesn't look up as I enter, but says:

'Have you, like, read this?'

'Yes, I have.'

She puts the book down and looks at me, and I experience a pleasant flutter in my tummy that is unrelated to my second tall latte.

'Starbucks!' Lea claps her hands, 'Where's the Starbucks, dude?'

'Baker Street. Not for the likes of you. You get the cafeteria brew. Now ... what are you doing here?'

'Just thought I'd say hi on my first day,' Lea hops down from my desk.

'Shouldn't you be with Alice?'

'Yeah. She's a character, isn't she? Is she actually an artist?'

'Yes, indeed, and a very talented one. She's also terrified of her students, so you should probably get on over there.'

'She's posh, isn't she?'

'Not really. Just well educated.'

'Same thing. Are you a writer?'

'No.'

'Alice says you are.'

'She's just being funny.'

'Alice is not funny. What, weren't you good enough?'

I say nothing, but take a step closer to the lovely Lea and find that she smells of vanilla. She's almost as tall as me, but still manages to gaze up from somewhere far below, with an inappropriate glint.

'Well, at least you've got your health, right?' And with that little gem, Lea is off.

As she leaves my classroom, she bumps into two boys from 9b, who step aside to let her pass.

'Hi there,' Lea says and saunters off, leaving the two to moon in her wake, mouths open.

Great. As if it's not difficult enough to keep their attention, now there's an attractive female on staff.

When I was a school student there was Mrs Beatrice Price. She was my homeroom and geography teacher, and all the boys jostled for her attention. All the boys, and I. I think Mrs Price was a subconscious factor to my getting into teaching. I remember her being very kind when my parents split up. I remember her telling me that it was okay if I wanted to have a little cry, and I remember making a real effort to weep in the hope that she'd hug me if I did.

After lunch, I manage to get the good seat, by the window, and am browsing through an old *Metro* when Alice joins me.

'How's your new assistant?' I ask, sipping my instant coffee, terribly casual.

'Lea is amazing. The kids love her.'

'I bet they do, the little pervs.'

'No, really. She gets through to them somehow. I feel truly comforted by her presence.'

Perhaps it is part of her artistic nature, but Alice will often say things like this, things that seem oddly intimate, and make people uncomfortable. She'll stop and think when anyone asks her how she's doing. Some people suspect her of also being gay, just because she's single and we happen to get on, but Alice loves men, though she's too flighty for monogamy. She dreams of the perfect love, but she can't be in a relationship. Alice says that it's the gap between what we want and what we can have that makes great art. That's why the most brilliant artists lose their minds; because of the desperation to believe that the ideals they produce in their work can cross the void to manifest in reality.

***

That Sunday I drive down to Richmond to see my mother and spend the day sitting in her garden drinking lemonade. I spend three hours in traffic on the way back. As I look for a space in the Tesco parking lot, I spot Lea Olvi on her mobile, her face twisted in distress. She's standing by a parked car and I barely recognise her. At first, I take her for a student. I drive past her twice, wondering if I should say something, and then leave Tesco and go to my local corner shop instead.

***

I get in early on Monday, and find Lea in the teachers' lounge smoking out the window.

'If Dexter sees you, she'll go postal,' I inform her.

'Fuck Dexter.'

'Is something the matter?'

Lea doesn't answer but tosses her cigarette butt out the window and marches past me.

I am left alone to contemplate the infinite moods of the human female.

A few hours later, the sun has yet again risen over Lea's disposition and she's laughing merrily while patrolling the yard with Mrs Patel.

She finds me in the teachers' lounge and takes a seat just a little bit too close.

'Hey, sorry about earlier. I had a mad weekend,' Lea takes a sip from my cup.

'Don't worry about it.'

We sit in silence for a while and I pretend to read the

paper; I pretend to read, while staring blindly at the page and issuing warnings to myself.

Stay away from the crazy straight girl.

Don't think about her warm thigh against yours; her vanilla scent, like a cupcake. Like those cupcakes my mother used to make when I was a kid, to store away, and give to me as a reward when I was a good girl. Bright pink icing that I used to eat off my fingers, until I was left with a naked sponge cup.

My good-girl cupcakes that I had to earn, and I have been such a good girl.

***

As the summer holidays approach, I find that I am bumping into Lea Olvi everywhere. I'm not sure if this is by happy coincidence or design, but everywhere I turn, there is she; in the yard, in the parking lot, by the shops, sitting in my classroom with her bare feet in my chair.

'People will talk,' I say, only half-joking, when I find her seated on my desk one morning. This time she is reading from a student's notebook, and from the glittery cover I know exactly whose notebook it is.

'You can't just read my student's work.'

'Shut up, I'm reading.'

I move her feet out of my chair and take a seat, waiting for her to finish Helen Lowie's poems. When she finally lowers the notebook, Lea is frowning.

'Who is this girl?' she asks me.

'Helen Lowie, my most committed pain in the arse,' I say.

'But she's really good. I mean, this is, like, beautiful,' Lea waves the notebook at me.

'I'm sure it's lovely.'

'Have you even read it?'

'Lea, this girl brings me a poem a week. And I have a job, which involves more paperwork than you can shake a rhyme at.'

'So, what, you just tell her to fuck off?'

And just like that, at eight seventeen on a Wednesday morning, I am having an argument with a hot woman about something other than what we're having an argument about.

'I can see that you are upset,' I say, soothingly.

'I'm not fucking upset,' Lea jumps off my desk and starts pacing about the classroom, her hands on her hips, face flushed, and though I know it's wrong, I can't help but get a little turned on.

'Why do you hate them?' she demands.

'I don't hate them, I think they are kids, and kids are difficult.'

'You hate them. You hate that they don't like the things you like. Like, I don't fucking know, Shakespeare and shit. You think they are scum. You can't even be bothered to read this girl's poems because you think they are all scum. People like you shouldn't be teachers. You know you're fucking up these kids, right?'

'You don't know anything about me,' I say, very slowly.

I can feel rage rising hot inside me, and I am determined to keep myself under control. She doesn't know anything about me. She's not been a teacher for seven years; she's not had to deal with all the bile.

'Just because you failed doesn't mean everyone else will ...'

I stand up, grab her by the arm and drag her out into the corridor. She doesn't make a sound but her face is a mask of fury and disgust. She reaches up to claw at me, but I slap her hand aside and leave her sitting on the floor. I turn to leave, but then turn back. She is looking up at me from the floor and I bend down to her and take her beautiful, angry face in my hand.

'You don't know a fucking thing about me,' I say again.

***

That Thursday afternoon, Alice bursts into my classroom, looking more flustered than usual. I'm packing up my stuff, getting ready to leave.

'Oh thank god, you're still here,' she says.

I ask her what's the matter and she asks if I finish early today. I tell her that I do, and Alice grabs hold of my sleeve with pure desperation. She tells me how she's supposed to take 7b to the National Gallery today and Mrs Patel was supposed to be the second supervisor, but she's off ill. And Mr Tomaki's got another two classes.

'I can't possibly go by myself with just Lea. I mean, she's great with the kids but it's 7b, you know how they are. Could you please, please ...?' she trails off and looks like she may fall into a faint.

After I have been to see Dexter and completed the four forms required of an off-premise supervisor, I join Alice, Lea and about half of the students from 7b. Lea smiles at me as we make our way to the tube stop.

On the train, passengers move seats to avoid us. Alice takes up post at one end of the carriage, and I take a seat at the other. Colin Archer and Samir Ali start a fight before we even get to Baker Street, and Alice has to threaten to pull the emergency brake.

Though she is like a little gazelle surrounded by a pack of lions, the kids seem to have respect for their art teacher. They don't ridicule her fear, or threaten her; they listen when she asks them to stop screaming, and they even listen when she tells them about feelings and the impressionist movement. She tells them how the impressionists sought to paint not what we see but what we feel. They were mocked for using colour and light instead of form, but what they accomplished was beyond what any movement ever had.

I begin to think that she is not as helpless as I have previously believed, and wonder at the source of her superpowers. Perhaps the kids respect the fact that she's an actual artist.

I share these thoughts with Lea, who is standing beside me.

'I don't think they give a shit that she's an artist,' Lea says, 'they don't get what she does. But, like, Alice loves art and loves making everyone else fall in love too. She actually gives a shit, and I guess they can tell.'

The group is more subdued at the end of our visit. Everyone's hungry and tired, and, after two hours of high art, I can't wait to get home and watch some trashy TV.

On the way down the marble steps leading from the gallery to Trafalgar Square, Colin Archer shouts out 'Lessie the Lesbo' and then pretends to look around for the culprit.

I ignore him, as I always do.

Lea, who is a few steps behind him, gives him a hard shove. The boy loses his balance and falls down the last few steps onto the pavement. I run down to make sure he's okay, while hoping no one else saw what I saw. Alice joins us just as Colin gets to his feet. She asks me what happened and I give her a shrug.

'She fucking pushed me,' he screams, pointing at Lea.

Tourists walk past and stare at us. It's a beautiful day and people are having their photos taken on the backs of the lions.

Alice tells Colin he must be mistaken.

'Yeah,' Lea says, 'you better watch your step, right. And your mouth.'

She's standing above the rest of us, fierce, ready for a fight. Colin looks like he wants to say something, but changes his mind and instead casts me a look of utter loathing.

Alice speaks gently to him, and starts herding the group down the street. Lea and I lag behind.

'Are you crazy?' I ask her.

'You can't just take that shit,' Lea says.

'Do you really think I care what a little brat has to say about me? You could have hurt him.'

'You can't just take that shit,' she says again, but this time she's smiling. With the sun full in her face, Lea is smiling like a little girl, and she takes my hand and gives it a squeeze.

I wonder who this woman is; who this girl is. I wonder why she wears her hair so short, and if she often gets into fights. I think about her dimples. For a moment I feel the power of a will greater than mine, greater than reason, wiser than wisdom.

It's crowded on the tube and we have to wait for a train that'll take us all. Finally on, we're packed in tightly, and I'm pressed up right against the doors. When the train gets to Baker Street, I feel a grip tighten on my arm and just as the doors are about to close, I am pulled off the train, onto the platform. As the tube begins to pull away, I look at Lea who's still holding my arm.

'Let's get coffee and then let's get a bottle of wine, and then let's go to yours.'

'Do you know what you're doing?' I ask her, knowing full well that it doesn't matter.

***

I leave Lea sleeping in my bed and get into school early the next day. I sit down at my desk and read Helen Lowie's glittery notebook once, and then again.

Then I sit very still for a long while and search for the part of me that went missing, I'm not sure when. I search and find it, lurking behind the walls I have raised to keep myself protected; walls that rose, disappointment by disappointment, while I was too scared, too lazy, to tear them down. I have spent most of myself clutching at the form, at the outline, of a life that never happened. I have preserved myself in amber, golden in my cage, numb but safe. And suddenly I feel a crack, and then another, and I see the flicker of possibilities beyond my imagination.

***

After my first class, I ask Helen Lowie to stay behind. I wait until everyone else has left and close the door.

'I'm sorry,' I say to her, terrified that I'll start crying. Helen gapes at me, her bag clenched to her chest.

'I am sorry that I've not been more supportive,' I say.

'That's alright, Miss,' Helen says, her face bright red.

'It is not alright. You are very talented, Helen. You really have a way with feelings, like … an impressionist.'

Helen looks at me like I may be mad, possibly dangerous, and I realise that I'm sounding like Alice.

'Look, I want to help you. I want to submit some of your work. See if we can get you published.'

'Oh, Miss …' Helen whispers, 'thank you so very much. You really like them?'

'I really do,' I say, and I really do.

I look for Lea at lunch but she's nowhere to be found. Alice tells me she's not been in, and that she had to clean up a pile of pink sick after Oliver Linberg dared Caz Allen to eat a tub of Carnelian oil paint.

Dexter interrupts my last class, just as I'm entertaining 7a with stories about famous writers and their fucked-up personal lives. I'm in the middle of giving a dramatic re-enactment of Virginia Woolf's death when Dexter enters my class and immediately kills the laughter.

'Read from your books,' she instructs them as she motions for me to exit with her.

We walk in silence through the hall and I get a bad feeling listening to her heels clip-clop ahead of me.

As we pass Marie at her desk, she gives me a constipated look of half-concern, half-disbelief.

'Lea Olvi,' Dexter finally says, closing the door behind her.

'Yes?'

'Do you know where she is?'

An image of her naked body, strong and so warm, drifts before me.

'No,' I reply, 'I don't think she was in today.'

Dexter takes a deep breath and sits down. She urges me to do the same, and I obey, grateful to live to tell another lie. Now, she looks to me like a concerned mother, weary and searching.

'What's the matter?' I ask.

'Mr Francis Allenton called us. He is Principal of St Martins Academy in Oxfordshire. His daughter's name is Julie Allenton.'

'Right ... I don't understand.'

'She ran away a few months ago. The police were called. I've spent two hours talking to a DC something or other. Good God, she's just seventeen years old.'

'Who is?'

'Who? Lea Olvi ... Julie Allenton, that's who. The girl stole her sister's passport. How could we have lost her?'

'Her sister? I'm sorry, I don't understand.'

'The older sister is a Leonora Olvi. Julie stole her passport. Someone recognised her at the National Gallery yesterday. They heard the name of the school and alerted the police. My God.'

'She is seventeen?'

'She is. Her father thought she was dead. He told me that.'

'Why did she run away?'

'I don't know, Nina, I don't care.'

When I get home an hour later there is no trace of Lea, of Julie. I try to call her mobile twice, and am about to hang up when her voicemail kicks in, but then I don't.

'Thank you,' I say. 'If you need anything … you know.' And I hang up.

Then I take out Helen Lowie's notebook and read it one more time.

Strays

The sun loomed above the cement blocks of the city, a bully in an empty playground, having now, at noon, chased away all shadows. It had not rained for four months and people, especially the old, had been dying for the past two weeks, most of them living in filthy homes on the outskirts of the capital. These were places where aged patients, turned out of hospital for being too well, went if they had nowhere else to go. During the siege of winter they had no heating for weeks at a time. Sometimes the one nurse begrudgingly assigned to each home forgot to bring the food allowance provided through a French charity. In one home, three inmates had been found dead, shrivelled like potpourri in the garden among the sage bushes they were tending. Apparently they had been caught out by the noonday heat and sat down for a moment's rest. By the time the nurse patrolling the home had found them only one had sufficient breath left to grab onto her plump arm with a trembling hand and, gazing up at the pink stern face, whisper: 'I want to go home ...' and 'Damn me, you are one ugly dog of a woman.'

It was just past noon, the traffic a slow drip through the artery leading from suburbia to the city centre. On the side of the road men in rough peasant's trousers and women in heavy skirts were selling watermelons from the back of carts. Stray dogs lurked on every corner, still in the heat and diffused by the rising dust. Mina felt resentful at where she had been brought and for a silent moment of indistinct thoughtlessness resented Lili for dying in this place.

Just that morning, she had been spread-eagled on the carpet of her living room, plucking at her bikini-line and watching Saturday morning TV.

Now in the cab, flung from side to side, Mina could feel the unfamiliarity like sharp fingers digging in her ribs. Outside, the heat rising from the asphalt gave the impression of puddles on the road ahead.

Mina could also feel something else; a sour guilt, making its way through her system like a bad meal. She had taken the earliest flight from London and had felt relieved to be leaving. A month away from work and Alice, even in this place, would be a good thing.

Alice, whom she had left looking like an orphan in a High Street Kensington Starbucks. Mina had arranged the meeting and selected Starbucks, knowing it would be packed on a Saturday. She' marched up and delivered her news with swift military efficiency. Alice had barely blinked; she had listened in silence, stirring her mug and watching people walking in and out. Mina had left her with a final 'I wanted you to know', then gone home and packed her bags. She had been annoyed at her friend's gentle acceptance, her sad little face, like she had nothing to say, or even worse: like she had always known it would happen. Like Mina's betrayal was barely a surprise.

A few hours later she was on the plane and while in the air she had felt at ease, almost light-headed, but as soon as the plane started its descent Mina remembered why she was returning.

At the airport she had jumped into the first cab that urged her in. She had replied in English when the driver asked whether she was here on holiday.

'For a funeral,' she'd told him, surprising herself.

The driver had only nodded in silence, but Mina felt exposed, and she continued the conversation quietly, with herself, in preparation.

'*Am fost tare ocupată cu viaţa mea,*' she said, over and over, until she was sure she had it right.

Her thighs were sticking to the plastic seat and she could see the driver looking at her through the rear-view mirror.

'You Romanian?' he asked, flicking a cigarette butt out the window.

'English.'

'No, no, English girls are pale and skinny.'

'Really.'

'English come for summer. Americans too. They come for the sea; they come for cheap holiday and act like pigs, make a mess and go back to New York and London and call us dirty.'

Mina took a deep breath and said nothing.

'You live in London?'

'Yes.'

'Nice, nice ... What do you do?'

'I am a doctor.'

Mina looked straight at the strip of face in the mirror. The driver's eyes had widened.

'Very good, very good.'

Though she knew the driver had charged her the tourist rate for the short ride, she paid without argument. There was plenty of time before her train so Mina walked around the station, at first in search of food and then of the toilets.

On her way to platform sixteen, a cluster of dirty

children gathered around her with their palms turned up and their whines a simple, constant onslaught. They followed her, jogging by her side, one even trying to sneak a little paw in her pocket, until her awkwardness flipped to annoyance and she finally snapped, 'Fuck the hell off.'

As she walked off she could hear them echoing 'fuck off, fuck off', and felt uneasy at hearing their childish voices rising behind her.

The train was ancient and dirty, but Mina was grateful to be on her way again. She watched the neglected city turn into countryside, and field after field of corn and sunflower drone by. She sneaked glances at the other five occupants of her compartment, wishing they would speak a bit slower. But their conversation was too quick for Mina to understand, and soon it was replaced by sleep.

Mina pulled out a magazine from her bag and kept it open on her lap. Her back was wet and her thighs were hot against each other. Her newly plucked bikini-line itched like hell, making her squirm in her seat, and then finally manage a great, half-discreet scratch under the magazine. Pale and skinny indeed, she thought as she dug her nails into her crotch feeling ripples of relief down her spine.

The train stopped and Mina looked out at the village; just a few low houses, tilting at random angles, some kids and dogs playing in the middle of the dirt road.

An uninvited thought of her mother came. So unexpectedly that at once Mina didn't know what to make of the fact, the fact sure to be pointed out to her, that she had not seen her mother for five years. Perhaps it wasn't that strange, she knew other people who rarely saw their parents. *Am fost tare ocupată cu viața mea*, she repeated again.

Mina's mum, Elena, had called her on a Saturday a few weeks ago to tell her the news. Mina had been having lunch with a friend and didn't pick up. On her way home she listened to the message and called Elena back, immediately feeling the guilt.

Lili was dead, Mina assured herself as the train started to move again. And what was done was done. The thing to do now, Mina thought, was focus on making it through the funeral, making it through a month in this place. Then she would go home and deal with Alice.

The woman opposite was awake now, her son, or perhaps grandson, curled up with his head in her spacious lap. She was eating sunflower seeds and spitting out the black little shells in her hand.

She looked straight at Mina examining her like a museum piece. Her hair was long and very dark, veined in grey and tied right at the nape of her thick neck.

'*Seceta*,' she said pointing with her chin. She spoke clearly, with a slow and articulate consideration that made Mina feel self-conscious.

Mina nodded.

'Look, no water.'

Mina looked out at the field passing close to the tracks.

'Dead,' the woman told her.

Outside hundreds of sunflowers bowed. All that should have been golden was brown; all that should have stretched towards the sun stooped in wilted defeat. They looked like a silent army of the beggar children Mina had seen at the station in Bucharest.

The woman ran a hand over the boy's hair; she smiled down at his sleepy murmur and then returned to her seeds and the view.

When night finally fell and the yellow halogen lights

came on in the carriage, Mina leaned over and asked the other question she had practised in her head.

'*Scuzaţi-mă, doamna, dar care este urmatoarea staţie?*'

The woman looked out.

'Next is Lacul Mare and after that Bogdan.'

Mina pulled down her suitcase, said thank you, and went to wait by the steel doors. When the train stopped she took the three steep steps onto the platform.

It was a warm black night, with the scent of burning wood and faded memory lurking below the stoop of the train house roof.

She walked through the hollow ticket hall, cracked porcelain tiles beneath her feet, and could see the large doorframe leading out onto the street. The frame stood vacant in the painted wall of the hall like a missing tooth. Rusty hinges told Mina that there must once have been a door. Through its absence she could see the headlights of a car draw nearer. She took out her mobile, hoping it would work, and wondering where the hell her mum was.

Mina stepped out onto the street. Three or four scabby dogs lay against the wall behind her, eyeing her with what could have been either curiosity or hunger.

The hairs on the back of her neck stood as the dogs rose from haunches to feet and ambled forwards.

'Mina!'

Mina turned and saw her mum approach, clapping and stomping at the advancing mutts. They stopped with low whines. Elena wrapped her arms around her daughter.

'You've lost weight. How was the journey?'

They walked to the car: a dusty Dacia, dented and resigned looking. Mina could tell her mum was still scared of driving; during all her years in London she had never once sat in the driver's seat, but when she'd moved back here necessity had forced her to drive more and more frequently.

'Do you recognise anything?' Elena asked in English.

'It's dark.'

'It's been a long time ... Too bad you should come back only because of ... of these sad things,' Elena said.

Last time Mina had seen her had been in a new Chinese restaurant in Richmond. When Mina had tried to take Alice there a few weeks ago it had been closed and the windows covered in brown paper. But with Elena, years ago, they had examined the dim sum menu under the golden ceiling decorations.

They had been shopping, and Elena was dealing with the disappointment of having to buy a size-twelve suit. Now, five years later, she looked like she'd shrunk back to a narrow ten. Her hair was cut short and, Mina knew, dyed a dark mahogany.

Elena stopped in front of a green iron gate and, on cue, Mina got out, opened the gate and stepped aside as her mum pulled into the yard.

Somewhere up ahead a dog was barking. There was a light in the kitchen window and over the flat roof Mina could make out the branches of the old bitter-cherry tree stretching out and up into the night. Elena stood with a hand on the small of Mina's back. The touch felt hot.

'I've left it to its own devices.' She gestured around the front yard, which in the night looked full. Mina walked up to the cement border and looked out, as to sea, over the clusters of flowers.

'Well, I've neglected it. Haven't had the time for gardening, but now you're here ...'

Mina followed her mum up to the house, wondering why her presence should make a difference. By the front door Elena pointed to the dog, chained to one side and barking wildly.

'This is Molly. She'll calm down once she gets used to you.'

Inside the kitchen Mina stopped and marvelled at how nothing had changed. Eighteen years had passed but the gas hob and table, set for two, and ancient wood-burning stove all stood their ground. Even the rug was the same, and Mina could see, under the table, the dark patch where she had lit a fire a long time ago.

Elena took her suitcase. 'I'll put this in the yellow room for you, you remember?'

On the hob were several pots and Mina opened a lid and peeked at the chicken soup inside, swirls of parsley on the surface and a large carrot poking out like a log.

Elena returned. 'Wash your hands and eat. *Haide.*'

When Mina was little Lili used to let her help make chicken soup. They would both go out into the backyard and pull out onions, carrots and potatoes, Lili waiting with a smile as Mina struggled with her onion. Then Mina got to pick a handful of parsley all by herself. Finally Mina watched as Lili caught one of the old hens and held it tightly under one arm with a blade in the other hand.

'I'm gonna do it, Mina-Lina-Catarina. You gonna watch?'

And Mina would cover her eyes and run away, returning a few hours later to the kitchen and a plate of hot soup.

'Did you kill it?' she'd ask, tearfully gazing at her bowl.

'No, no, strange thing, Mina-Lina-Catarina, when you left the poor thing just died in my arms.' Lili would smile, and Mina would eat.

Mina felt a wave of exhaustion and let her spoon drop from her hand. Elena reached out and touched her.

'You tired?'

'I think I'm just going to go to sleep. The soup was lovely, thanks.'

Elena got up and led the way. Though the house was much like the kitchen, unchanged, Mina had the feeling she'd get lost if left on her own.

'We just got back the hot water.'

Next to the bathroom was Mina's room. Elena had opened her suitcase and hung up her black dress. This used to be her grandmother's room before it was turned into a spare with yellow walls. The main light didn't work, and only a dim lamp on the bedside table lit the room.

On the bed lay an old-fashioned nightgown, pink, lacy and full-length. 'Sexy,' Mina held it up.

'You'll be the belle of the ball, my love,' Elena said in English and sat down with a sigh. Outside the dog was still barking. The night, drifting in through the opened window, was settling in the corners of the room and gathering like smoke against the ceiling.

'I'm happy you're back, Mina. Happy.'

Mina sat down and didn't look at her mum. Her tired mum, with the corners of her mouth drooping even more than she remembered.

'I'm happy too.'

'It's taken you too long, angel. Too long.'

That was Mina's cue.

'*Mama. Am fost tare ocupată cu viața mea.*'

'This is your home too, Mina. This is part of your life.'

'Yes, but I have been busy with my life. My life in London ...'

It sounded weak in English.

Her mother's shoulder grazed hers as Elena breathed in and out.

'You still smoke?' Mina asked.

'Oh angel, I'll never stop now. You?'

'Nah.'

The lamp on the bedside table flickered and Mina suddenly asked, 'Where did Lili die?'

'What?'

'In which room? Did she die here?'

Elena stood up with a strained look. She smoothed the sides of her dress and took a step into the arch of the doorway.

'Why? She just died ... She is dead. It wasn't in this room, don't worry.'

Mina raised her eyebrows.

'How's your friend, Alice?'

'Yeah, fine. She's fine. Look mum, I'm going to get ready for bed.'

***

The following morning Mina awoke with her mum leaning over her. She was wearing the black House of Fraser suit that she had bought in Richmond during her last visit to London. Her hair was up and her face round and pale, the blusher like a slap on each cheek. She whispered gently as to a sleeping child.

'Mina, it's six, I have to go meet the priest. Can you make it to the church by yourself or do you want me to pick you up here at nine?'

Mina stretched and sat up. The morning was cool and bright, and after the hot and black night it came as a gift.

'I'll be fine, I'll just ask someone. It's just down the road, right?'

'I'll have my phone with me.'

Elena handed her a piece of paper with her mobile number, the name and address of the church, and the address of their house – 'Bogdan, Romania' – written in brackets.

Mina laughed. 'Thanks mum, in case I take a wrong turn and end up in Bulgaria?'

'Be at the church by nine thirty. Nine thirty.'

Elena kissed Mina on the cheek and left the room, closing the door carefully behind her. Alone again, Mina waited until she heard her mum leave the house and then got up.

The tables in the living room and kitchen had been set with crisp white tablecloths. Two piles of plates, her mum's best china, a few rows of crystal glasses and a bunch of silver spoons all waited prettily for the mourners. Nothing stirred, nothing welcomed. Mina poured herself a glass of water and, leaning on the low enamel sink, gulped it down. The water tasted different here, sweeter.

Back in the yellow room she lay down again and fell asleep.

When she awoke, Molly was barking, pulling her chain across the yard. It was hotter now, the ease of the morning gone. Mina stretched; she had barely moved in her sleep and her neck was sore. She went over to the window and stood looking out through the green mosquito net that was stapled to the frame.

When her gaze fell on the clock ticking on the bedside table, she was jolted into action, and almost screamed in shock. She threw off the nightgown, pulled on the dress and shoes, grabbed her bag and rushed out.

As she locked the door Mina ran her fingers through her hair trying to catch a final glimpse of herself in the glass panels.

By the front gate the stone lips of an old well pursed. Mina stopped by it and hovered on the edge of memory. It came like a taste in her mouth, rising from her throat and for a moment clouding her eyes. It was the heavy aroma of white tobacco flowers. It was summer, a long time ago. All the summers of long ago, Mina would stand on her tippy-toes staring down the well at the play of light on the cool surface below. They were one of the first families to get running water, to the eternal jealousy of Doamna Ionescu, their neighbour, and though there was no need for it anymore, the well remained at the front of the garden. Every year Mina had to look further and further down to find the surface. Lili had told her the earth was sucking the water back down again. She'd sneak up behind Mina and pinch her sides, making her jump. 'Ai,' she'd say laughing, 'ai, ai, don't you fall in girl, or you'll be falling forever. Don't you know this well is magic?' She'd sit down with Mina, their backs against the rough stones, looking out over the roses and marigolds and flowering sage bushes.

Mina sat down. She looked out over the weeds, shadowless in the high sun. It was past eleven now. The ceremony would soon be over; there was no point. Her mum would be back with friends and family for the wake. The house would be full of strangers remembering Mina as a child and wanting to know how she was doing. Wanting to hear of her success. The success she had built over the years in her stories to her mum, and which her mum had proudly rendered to everyone else.

Mina leaned her head back and gave a great laugh. She laughed, unable to stop, until her eyes were filled with tears. Lili, her aunt, her second mum, the one she had loved deeply and loyally from childhood to adulthood, was to be buried in only a matter of minutes. Mina had come all the way back for a funeral she was missing.

A month ago Mina had told her mum of a promotion.

She had told her of a glass-walled office and a sulky but efficient PA, devoted to Mina's every wish. A few days later Mina had received an envelope. Inside was a cheap-looking postcard with a photograph of yellow flowers on the front and on the back written in Romanian, in a strained, illegible hand, were a few lines. With the postcard came a note from her mother:

> *Congratulations from Lili. She writes: 'All*
> *my love to you, my Mina-Lina-Catarina.*
> *You have done well far away. I miss you*
> *every day and hope to see you.'*

She'd died the following week, peaceful in the knowledge that Mina-Lina-Catarina was doing well for herself.

At the heart of Bogdan was its cemetery. Sprawling and mostly neglected, it was an equal distance from the fields to the north and east as to the train track to the south and the woods to the west. By the main entrance, on either side, there had once been a group of ancient chestnuts huddled together, their thick trunks black and hollow, but they were cut down to make room for more graves. Now the cemetery lay flat, not a tree in sight, only the two churches rising above the tombstones.

The smaller, Catholic, church, which Mina was heading towards, had been built by two Bohemian brothers in the late nineteenth century. The larger, Greek Orthodox, one was much older and from a distance it looked like a miniature cathedral. These were two of the few churches not demolished during the many years of communism, and they even attracted a handful of tourists during the summer months. At one point all four exterior walls of the Orthodox building had been covered in bright paintings, in an attempt to mimic the famous monasteries of the north. Now only the southern fresco was still clear, while the other three were speckled with bursts of colour and the occasional head or arm. One time, someone had added to the floating head of Christ a female torso, complete with a huge pair of tits. The nipples had been joined by a chain of rude words written in neat block letters. It had caused great outrage, and Doamna Ionescu had embarked on a campaign to find the perpetrators and bring them to justice.

Mina remembered walking through the quiet cemetery with Lili, in between the hollow chestnuts, feeling magic. Now, all she could feel was a hot liquid fuss in her belly. She was two hours late.

She stopped in front of the great wooden door and listened to the muffled voices inside. 'I can't fucking believe this,' she whispered to herself.

Doubt gripped Mina, but as she turned to leave the door opened with a smack of cold air. The priest's voice, now loud and deep, echoed brilliantly and uninterrupted. The sunshine from outside lit the stained glass windows high above, but didn't reach the pews or the faces that now turned to her. Mina walked to the front row, guessing her mother would be there. With every step her heels gave hollow clonks. She sank down, feeling slightly nauseous.

Next to her, Elena stared dead ahead. She didn't even blink as her daughter sat down, offering an embarrassed smile. She hunched, swallowed by her suit, in the belly of the church, seemingly unaware of anyone else.

It was a small church, and only ten wooden pews lined the centre, but the hollow above them seemed eternal to Mina, the painted ceiling lost in gloom. Next to them, across the centre aisle, Doamna Ionescu's beady little eyes held Mina in steady judgement. At first Mina wasn't sure – this woman looked more like Doamna Ionescu's mother, frail and wispy – but as the eyes narrowed and the lips curled into a thin smirk there could be no doubt. This was an old Doamna Ionescu.

It surprised Mina that she should be here. To her knowledge, the last time Doamna Ionescu and Lili had spoken was over thirty years ago.

Lili had been caught standing by their gate, where Doamna Ionescu swore she saw her 'casually chatting to some gypsy'. She was returning home and spotted Lili tossing her head in laughter while the man ran his fingers through his black hair. Doamna Ionescu spent the rest of the week retelling the story in various states of outrage.

'I tell you it's as true as the grave! I saw her with my own eyes: standing on the street, no troubles, sticking out her flat chest and laughing. Hahahaha! Like a teenager.'

The priest's voice droned on, soft and deep, and Elena's hand grabbed onto Mina. Mina jumped in surprise and looked at her mother. Elena's mouth was stretched across her teeth in muted pain. Her eyes were pleading, brimming with tears. When she spoke it was a low moan, too deep for her small frame, and Mina looked up at the hollow above in search of the source.

'Oh Lili … Poor Lili.'

She whispered hotly against her daughter's cheek.

'Mina, forgive me, I let her die alone in that awful, awful place.'

A few people had turned in their seats and were looking in their direction. Mina hushed her mother soothingly, but Elena went on, in English, calmly now.

'She … left. She just left the house and I didn't go after her, because I was angry. No, not angry... tired. I found her two days later in a home. They had plucked her off the street and she died in the heat. She couldn't remember where she lived. She died.'

Mina thought of Lili, alone in her final moments.

Elena leaned back and was wiping her face. Mina moved closer to her.

'Mami. I shagged Alice's boyfriend. I have been fucking my best friend's guy for over a year. Over a year. And I don't really feel bad. Just annoyed that he still loves me. And I hate her for not hating me, for not screaming at me, for just being... sad.'

Elena froze, hand poised with the tissue. Their eyes met, Elena's wide with surprise, and they both gave a loud sigh.

Then Mina felt her mouth twitch and she saw her mother shake her head and smile, and she had to look away.

She looked up at the priest and tried to focus on the sermon, on the deep voice, on the faces of people she might have known. She tried to forget what she had just learned.

There would be time to remember.

Fig

It was a quiet night. A light, warm, summer night.

It was Sunday, around eleven thirty. Not that Clari had a view to a clock, but she knew it must be around eleven thirty, on a Sunday night, by Mark's enthusiastic plodding on top of her.

Mark was one of the three things Clari knew, beyond certainty, belonged to her. He had been her property – or, more generously, her boyfriend – for thirty-two weeks; yes, she counted the weeks. She knew the days and hours as well, but preferred not to think of these. Mark was loyal, kind and loving, and if it were not for his remarkable resemblance to a male of the human species, might very well have passed for a labrador puppy.

Mark ended each conversation with 'I love you' and remembered the anniversary of their first meeting, first kiss, first shag, first holiday, and counting. Only a few months ago, when Clari had been enraged by something trivial but remarkably potent, and told him to please get the fuck out of her house, he had stopped mid-sentence with a soft look dawning on his face and said, 'Babe, you know this is the first time you've thrown me out?'

To which Clari responded, reasonably, by throwing a mug (decorated with kittens, and belonging to him, not her) at his head.

The second thing Clari knew belonged to her was the two-up two-down, semi-detached, ten-minutes-from-the-tube property, bequeathed to her by a semi-unknown, much-appreciated auntie. The woman had apparently had no children of her own, and might also have been a small yet perfectly formed fruit-loop as she, in her will, had left her Tufnell Park property to 'the oldest child of her youngest sister's niece'.

Clari had moved into the house some four years previous and had for the past six months rented out the ground floor to a woman named Katja.

Katja was something of an enigma, wrapped in a mystery, wrapped in a tatty old shawl. She was Russian mostly, but on a couple of occasions had referred to a childhood in Hungary and a romantic misadventure in Milan. She might have been anything between thirty-five and fifty-five years old and, though not the least bit attractive, had a kind of hypnotic appeal with her ridiculously long hair and huge tits.

And they were huge.

They were the kind of tits a prepubescent boy comes across in an old '60s porn mag and is immediately and irrevocably turned gay.

Katja also hated cats, and Clari had come home one evening to find her tenant hissing, actually hissing, at their neighbour's kitty, a bright orange tom named Dick. Clari had gaped incredulously at the woman, who had simply said, 'He started it,' and turned away.

Dick vanished, mysteriously, a few weeks later and poor Mrs Velda, their old neighbour, put up posters all over the street. The posters showed an orange cartoon cat with huge eyes. Mrs Velda had chosen the cartoon cat because she did not have any photos of Dick, and was deeply disturbed by the onslaught of creative vandalism the posters elicited from her neighbours. In a few days every one of the cartoon kitties had been equipped with tits and cocks of infinite variety, comedy glasses, mohawks, bottles of booze, Hitler moustaches and one quite random doodle of a snake, which Clari suspected her tenant was responsible for.

Clari didn't mind weirdos as such, and Katja always paid her rent on time, by direct debit. What was, however, a bit worrying was the fact that, since the day Katja had moved in, she had played host to a ceaseless chain of visitors who knocked on her door at almost any time of the night and day. There were men and women, young and old, some looking furtive and distinctly artistic, others looking like lost bankers. There were the respectable ladies in their beige outfits and expensive perfume, which wafted up the stairs to Clari.

There were also the earthier footballer's-wife types, with platinum blonde locks, who clonked about in their sky-high platform heels making the very foundation rattle and forcing Clari to put a sign on the front door requesting: 'Visitors to please remove shoes'.

During the first week, Clari had thought these to be the weird woman's weird friends. She tried to ignore the issue for a whole month, during which more sinister suspicions took root.

Finally, no longer able to suppress her qualms, Clari knocked on Katja's door, half-dying of curiosity and half-determined to kick her dubious arse out.

The woman opened the door a few inches and stuck out her head, fixing a pair of dark eyes on her landlady.

'You knock?' she said.

'Yes, I did ... may I come in?'

'No, this is not good time.'

Clari's eyes narrowed as she fought the urge to tell the

little bitch that, as it was her house, she would determine when was a good time.

'Look, I would like to have a word with you.'

'Yes?'

'How do I put this ... are you a whore?'

At this, Katja let out a hail of laughter and stepped out from behind her door, her bazooms forcing Clari to take a step back.

'I am not whore.'

'Oh good. You're just very popular?'

'I run business, but it is not sex.'

'Right.'

'I am witch.'

'Pardon ... you are which what?'

'No, no ... I am *a* witch.'

'Right. As in spells and stuff?'

'Yes. Is that problem?'

Clari considered, and then shrugged, 'No, I don't mind. I've got gypsy blood, you know, on my mother's side. She used to read palms and all that stuff.'

And Clari really didn't mind. She even took pride in having a Russian witch living with her and mentioned this casually to people, to increase her quirky factor.

But it was Sunday evening, Mark was happily pounding along, praising the Lord and clearly close to creating a wet spot on Clari's newly washed sheets, when she reached a climax of sorts, a conclusion.

She shoved him off, sat up in bed and watched his sweaty, pasty, confused form with a feeling of having stepped in dog shit.

'What, baby? What's the matter?' he huffed, 'Did I hurt you?' he added reaching out and caressing Clari's arm.

She swatted him aside. 'No ... Look, we need to talk.'

And she told him. She told him how every time she heard his voice it was like being doused with icy water, and that the only reason she let him fuck her every Sunday night was because there was nothing good on the telly, and that the moment the BBC or Channel 4 reconsidered their appalling Sunday line-up, he would have to contend himself with a quiet wank in the loo, and before that happened it would be better to just call it a day, wouldn't it?

He looked at her with his labrador eyes, his lip trembling, and asked, 'Do you hate me?'

And here Clari performed her greatest act of kindness, and said, 'No, I don't hate you, I'm just feeling a bit stifled. I'm sorry, Mark, you really are very... sweet,' she patted his bare shoulder and smiled. 'Do you think you could get your stuff out by next week?'

He looked away, but said, 'I'll have my brother pick it up.'

'You have a brother?' Clari asked, and Mark dashed out of bed and into the bathroom, where he locked himself in for the rest of the night, forcing Clari to wee in a terracotta flowerpot on the balcony.

**

The next morning Mark was gone.

Clari went to work.

Work: this was the third thing Clari knew to be her own.

And work was close to Bow station, in an old warehouse, in the new, plush offices of *Art Now* magazine, where Clari was employed as a subeditor. She had worked for *Art Now* since its birth, three years ago – first as a receptionist, then as an administrator and finally as a sub.

She had once tried to explain to a drunken stranger at a party how it felt to walk into the lively, bright office with all the young, beautiful, ambitious people and watch their collective talents congeal into the living thing that was *Art Now*. It felt like belonging to something, like being part of a club or something.

'It's basically a pretentious student rag? I mean, does anyone actually buy it, for money?' asked the drunken idiot.

Art Now was nothing like a student paper. It was cutting-edge journalism, dealing with art and life and all kinds of super important stuff. But yes, the magazine's actual owner happened to be a student, a very rich student, whose father was a Lord something or other, and who often decorated the pages of other, lesser magazines, and who was, should the truth be told, already growing bored of this particular venture.

And yes, there had been a few misses, a few professional lapses, like when the *t* had accidentally been omitted from the name of the magazine, on issue number eight, forever prompting idiots to go around crying, '*Arrr Now*, me matie!'

Then there had been that one time when Des, their resident stud freelancer, had plagiarised a whole article on, ironically, copyright and the arts. Clari chose to believe that it had been an intentionally subversive act, a kind of postmodern attempt to draw attention to a very real and disturbing issue. She did, however, refrain from using the word postmodern, the drunken arsehole's accusation still fresh on her mind.

Des had simply explained away his little booboo with osmosis. There are no original ideas, he had said, every artist soaks up and regurgitates the work of others.

And Des got away with it, like he got away with everything.

Des had, and this was fact, shagged every woman in the office (excluding Clari) and two of the men. He was a kind of weedier version of Russell Brand, and he seemed to have an informed, usually highly amusing, opinion on every topic. He treated everyone like shit, which was an essential part of his appeal.

Clari had never much fancied Des. But on this day, in the wake of her break-up, unexpectedly and irresistibly, she did.

And when he stopped by her desk, leaned in and asked, as he often did, 'So, you fancy it?' Clari shrugged.

That night Des took Clari out for a drink. He talked about himself for a straight hour and called Clari 'Clair'.

Finally, he said, 'You know, I thought you had a boyfriend.'

'I did.'

'And?'

'We decided to go our separate ways.'

'You dumped him, then. You seem like the kind of girl who dumps her boyfriends. Actually, you don't seem like the kind of girl who has boyfriends.'

Clari neither confirmed nor denied the accusation. She said nothing, which wasn't a problem as he soon began talking about himself again. And she was just about to tune out, to write the whole night off as a waste of her time, when Des reached under the table, swiftly found his way under her skirt and inside her pants, and began fingering her, right there at the corner table of the King's Arms.

He whispered, 'And who's a wet little whore then?' and then continued with his random chitchat while wrist-deep inside Clari.

That night Des fucked Clair, there was no doubt about that. It started on the train on the way back to hers, and continued until the small hours of the morning. He had her begging him to keeping going and to stop and to keep going, he had her screaming and whimpering, he had her from the back, the side, the front, the top, performing acrobatic feats she had never thought herself capable of.

When Clari woke up late the next morning Des had vanished and it was too late to go into work, so she called in sick and walked about her flat luxuriating in the freshly screwed feeling, making herself an elaborate lunch and drinking cup after cup of fresh coffee.

She went downstairs to check the mail and bumped into Katja in the hallway. Katja gave Clari a wry smile.

'Good morning,' said Clari, feeling her ears go red.

'Morning. I think you were popular too, last night, yes?'

Clari ignored this and went back upstairs, where she had a bath and noticed that most of Mark's belongings had been removed and that only two boxes, bearing his name, remained cowering in a corner of the hall.

By the early evening Clari began feeling restless.

She stood holding her phone for a few minutes before dialling Des's number.

'Yes?' he answered.

Clari put on her most seductive voice. 'So ... do you fancy it?' she purred.

'Erh ... no, not really,' Des said.

'Pardon?'

'Hey look, let's be adult, right? You're a lot of fun and everything, but our time is up.'

'What time?'

'Our time, babe. See you around.'

And he hung up.

***

Over the next few days Clari launched a full dirty war against Des. She paid an old friend, who worked at a club and was thus up until the small hours, to call Des every hour, for the whole night, and just breathe. She edited his copy creatively, including a whole extra paragraph on the benefits of recreational drugs and how best to score them. Though she was disappointed to find that not only were people not outraged, they actually congratulated him on a brilliant piece.

But at home, alone, she decided that she didn't want things to get nasty with Des, they had to work together after all, and so she called him and left a friendly little message on his phone, saying that she thought he was alright and that she hoped they might be mates.

When he didn't call her back, Clari called him again and left a less kind message, and by the seventh message the tone had definitely deteriorated from friendly to threatening.

She read her horoscope. It said, 'Do not set your expectations too high.' She didn't much like this, and so she read all the other horoscopes until she found one she did like ('What you long for can be yours with a little perseverance').

She took this as a sign to call Des again.

A few hours later and Clari was standing outside Katja's door, hand poised, about to knock, but holding back.

'This is crazy,' she said to herself, but before she could say anything else, the door opened and Katja stood before her, wearing all black, her eyes sparkling wickedly.

'Knock, knock?' said the woman, helpfully.

Clari lowered her hand.

'I was wondering ...' she started.

'I will help,' Katja interrupted, turned and sashayed back into her flat, trailing beads and shawls and long oily hair. Clari followed and found herself stepping into a kind of New Age brothel, all red velvet furnishings, candles, heavy curtains, and, on a purple velvet chaise longue, a bright orange furry cushion.

Clari stared at it.

'Oh my god … is that Dick? Is that Mrs Velda's cat?'

Katja patted the cushion fondly and smiled.

'I make everything myself,' she said proudly, 'curtains, candles, tablecloth, everything. With my own hands.'

Clari nodded, her eyes fixed on poor Dick, the former tom, and now the cushion cover.

'And now… business,' Katja said. She sat down at a table in the middle of the room, and Clari took the seat opposite.

'Give me hands,' Katja said, and Clari did as she was told, thinking that perhaps the time had come to read fortunes. But instead the Russian grabbed her hands hard just below the wrist and held them while looking straight into Clari's eyes.

'What you want?'

Clari sighed. 'Des.'

'This man doesn't want you?'

'No.'

'You want to make him?'

'Yes.'

There was a silence, a heavy, awkward silence. Clari tried to pull her hands away, but could not.

'Okay, I'll help you. Three hundred pounds off next month rent.'

'Three hundred? Are you crazy? I'll give you a hundred off.'

'Three hundred.'

'What if it doesn't work, then? Two hundred.'

'Three hundred, and if it doesn't work it wasn't meant to be.'

'Well that's bloody convenient. Fine, three hundred. But I want Dick too. The cushion,' Clari pointed.

An hour later Clari was back in her own flat.

She stood in the hall holding one ripe fig in her hand and glaring at it. It was simple, Katja had said, this spell had been used by women in the Middle East for thousands of years. Since the days of old this little piece of volatile magic had brought back wayward husbands and won the love of heroes.

It was really very simple: the woman is to store the fig for three full days and nights, and then bake her man a cake with it. After this, he will never want another woman.

'Store it where?' Clari had asked.

'Inside you,' said Katja, smiling, 'Inside, you know...'

Clari now stood pinching the fig between thumb and forefinger.

Quickly, so as not to have time to change her mind, she pulled down her jeans, and her panties, and carefully, trying not to squash it, inserted the fruit like a soft, weirdly shaped tampon.

'Three days,' she sighed, straightening up.

For the next three days and nights the fig lived inside Clari. She tried not to think about it too much, and instead went about her business as usual. At work she ignored Des, who seemed hugely grateful.

At home she researched cake recipes and tried to ignore the itching.

On the Sunday, after the full three days, Clari was standing in her kitchen, sugar, flour, milk and butter lined up before her, the oven on at 200°C and a cake tin greased and ready. She was wearing a t-shirt and a pair of socks, her bottom was bare and slightly cold, and she finally reached down for the last ingredient.

***

Clari had pulled on a pair of jeans, and was taking her work of art out of the oven. She sniffed it suspiciously: it smelt okay. She considered how great it would be if she could try it out on someone first, on someone who didn't matter, just to see if it worked, if it was safe.

Katja had told her that, on very rare occasions, the festering fig could make the recipient a bit ill.

'How ill?' asked Clari.

And Katja had smiled and shrugged, indicating that it was almost never fatal.

The front door buzzer went off, and for one moment she thought that maybe the spell had worked just like that.

She pressed the intercom, and whispered, 'Hello?'

'Is that Clari?' asked a stranger's voice. 'This is Eric, Mark's brother. I've come for his boxes.'

Clari stood gazing into space for a moment, feeling the annoyance build inside her. How dare he, she thought wildly, come here and interrupt me…And she stopped, smiling to herself, and pressed the button again.

'Of course, Eric, but do come in.'

A few minutes later, Eric, who was a taller, slightly fatter, version of Mark, stood in her hall, trying not to meet Clari's eyes.

'I am sorry about all of this,' she said, looking forlorn.

'Yeah, well…Is that his stuff?' Eric pointed at the boxes in the corner and took a step towards them.

Clari sidestepped in front of him. 'It really is great of you to come and do this, Eric. Thank you so much.'

Eric nodded, and again attempted to reach the last of Mark's remnants. Again, Clari blocked his path.

'It has been just so hard for me…'

Eric shrugged.

'Would you like a cup of tea?'

Here Eric did look into her eyes, and they were

huge and honeyed and brimming with tears, and before he knew how it had happened, he found himself seated in a sofa, being brought a cup of tea by Clari, who really was not the evil bitch his brother had portrayed her as.

She placed the cup before him and smiled, prettily.

'Cake?' she asked.

***

At *Art Now*, it was someone's birthday. A blonde, skinny someone, who had screamed 'Like oh my god I'm so fucking old!' when the office had presented her with a giant birthday card, bearing '22' in large red numbers.

A chocolate cake, covered in sticky white icing, had been chopped up and distributed. Des, who had come in especially to wish the birthday girl well, had helped himself to a slice, placed it on his desk, and then strolled off to see what plans the blonde had for the evening.

Clari took her chance and surreptitiously got up from her desk. She strolled, casually, to Des's cubicle, holding in her hand a piece of cake wrapped in foil. She unwrapped it quickly and with a plastic fork lifted the icing off Des's slice and plastered it on hers. She placed her cake on the little paper plate, ditched the other, and then went back to her seat, waiting.

Her mobile rang, just as she watched Des retuning to his desk.

It was Mark. She ignored it.

Des was smiling at an email he was reading, typing something back with enthusiasm. She watched him pull the paper plate closer to him.

The blonde stopped by his desk. Des showed her something on his computer screen and they both laughed, him in a masculine baritone, her in a girly shrill.

Des whispered something to her, and she hit his shoulder playfully.

Clari's mobile beeped and, in an attempt to distract herself, she picked it up to listen to the voicemail she really couldn't care less about.

For one irrational moment, the idea of hearing Mark's voice felt comforting. And then she heard it, trembling on her voicemail, and was immediately annoyed.

The blonde was now sitting in Des's lap. They were typing something together, while she giggled helplessly.

'Clari...' Mark's voice sobbed, 'Clari, my brother, Eric, he's in the hospital ... he really isn't well, I need to know...'

Clari pressed delete. She put the mobile down.

She watched the blonde wriggle back to her desk.

She watched Des take a large forkful of her special cake. She half-stood in her chair and reached out towards him, about to yell something, when he gave her a look: a tiny dirty glance filled with pure contempt.

Clari sat back down.

She watched the fork get closer to his mouth, and for one moment thought to herself, 'He'll either want me again or he'll get what he deserves.'

But then Clari let out a howl, jumped to her feet, clambered over her own desk, scattering computer monitor, papers, stapler to the floor and, still screaming, propelled herself at Des, slapped the fork out of his hand, grabbed the paper plate off his desk and threw it into the bin and, for good measure, shoved her foot in the bin and stomped on it.

She thought, 'I am a good person, I am a fucking good person and I am not going to let a man possibly die even though he deserves it.'

She stopped screaming and looked around; the whole

office had freeze-framed and was watching her with varying expressions of shock and confusion. The blonde had a look of dazed alarm on her face, which, Clari noted with annoyance, suited her.

Des had shrunk back in his chair and looked properly scared; properly five-year-old-lost-in-the-supermarket-monsters-under-the-bed-that-film-with-the-zombies-that-kill-everyone-and-will-get-you terrified.

As Clari was leaving the office a few minutes later, possibly for the last time, she felt proud of herself. Yes, she had probably lost her job and a little bit of her dignity, but she had also saved a man's life.

Her mobile started ringing again and this time she answered.

'Look, Mark, I'm really sorry. About your brother, I mean. I can't really explain but I was, you know… I feel responsible.'

'No, no, it's …' Mark started, but Clari interrupted him.

'Maybe the doctors need some … information … maybe, I don't know, but I am sorry. It's my fault.'

'It really isn't,' Mark whispered.

'No, it really is,' Clari insisted.

'No, Clari, you had nothing to do …'

'Look, Mark, believe me, it was my fault.'

'How could it have been? I mean, if that driver…'

'That what now?' Clari stopped.

'The driver of the bus? Clari, Eric was run over by a double-decker in Camden. What did you think?'

Clari didn't answer, but stood watching the road, thinking that a double-decker might not be a bad way to go after all; thinking that of all the things she had thought were hers, only one remained and it didn't seem like much.

Drop

We are waiting for the bottom to drop. We are waiting under the dome of a perfect sky, with the heat in our eyes, sweat down our backs and suspicion rising somewhere beyond the horizon.

The waiting began as soon as we left London, left it behind in a blaze of glorious late summer, with Eli moaning that we were to miss those few precious days every year when London is a sweet-tempered delight.

Radio 4 warns that the Indian summer we've been enjoying is sure to end, with gloom to follow, and Eli smacks her lips and switches off to silence. She says it is the same as telling a happy someone their joy is sure to curdle eventually; why take it away from them? Why not allow the nation to plan barbecues and hang their laundry out to dry? Why worry about the rain that always falls when it isn't falling yet?

'To taper expectations,' I say, for argument's sake.

'Bullshit. Disappointment is always disappointing.'

I glance at her, trying to spot any hidden meaning, but Eli is gazing out the window at the passing countryside, already lost in a blur of green and gold. That's what disappointment is to her; a passing blur, insubstantial and vague.

We stop at a BP station to fill up the car and buy snacks, and Eli insists we get a tub of Ben & Jerry's Chunky Monkey. The attendant is a tall, thin young man. He wears the regulation green shirt, and smiles as if expecting the world to laugh at him. His nametag says 'Jamie'.

Jamie gives me a nod and a grunt.

'How's it going, mate?' I ask, in a low, gentle tone.

I wonder, for no reason, about his life; if he lives in the country and if he's still a virgin. My dad once told me that a man always looks people in the eye. I wonder what pearls of wisdom Jamie has gotten from his folks.

'Ice-cream,' he says, smiling at Eli.

Eli nods.

'Where you heading, then?'

'Devon.'

'That's nice, that's really nice.'

'You should come along, Jamie,' Eli flirts shamelessly, leaning forward on the counter. Jamie's gaze flutters from her to me and back to her, his whole body erect, his smile uncertain, as well it should be.

'Yeah, like?'

'Oh yeah. We're going camping. I hate camping. Do you hate camping, Jamie?'

'I ... I ...'

'We're going camping because my mate here thinks it will help cure me.'

'Are you ... ill?'

Eli laughs and takes my hand, placing it against her mouth.

'Very,' she says into me.

When we get back to the car, Eli jumps into the backseat, stretches out amongst the mess and falls asleep within minutes. The old Volvo is packed with boxes and bags, everything Eli owns in the world. I glare at the ancient PC, now on the seat next to me, and wince at the vicious bastard.

Time passes and all I know is the dark slit between her parted lips as she lies sleeping.

We get into Modbury and drive for an hour before we finally find the campsite. The ice-cream has turned to mush and Eli drinks it out of the container. I'm unloading the tent, trying to decide which way is south.

'That's so fucking nasty,' I tell her.

Eli scoops up a Chunky Monkey and throws it at me.

Though summer is drawing to an end, and the trees are blushing with the advancing change, the place is chocker. All around the campsite tents of absurd dimensions have popped into being out of the copious interiors of the four-wheel drives that seem to be the only acceptable way of getting into the wilderness.

***

I am reading the Culture section of last Saturday's *Guardian*, my feet are bare in the sun, and I am massaging the grass with my toes. The nail on my left big toe is a stunning purple-black shade of agony.

Eli is lying topless in the sun, on her stomach, tanning herself.

I notice that the large fella next to us, with his executive tent and plump family, has noticed this. He is working on his fifth can of lager and keeps reaching greedy glances towards Eli. His daughter, of whom he is blissfully unaware, is howling by his side, her face red and her little fat fists clenched. The kid, who is no more than six years old, is prostrate with the grief of being denied a third ice-lolly and shrieking for all she is worth, tugging at her father's shorts.

Eli is listening to her iPod, singing lazily, and out of key, along to Madonna's 'Holiday'.

She pulls an earphone out and glares towards our neighbour, her abrupt movement offering a flash of creamy delight.

'You think someone's gonna shut that kid up?' she says.

'You shut up. You want her father to eat you? Look at the size of him.'

We laugh and glance towards the man, who has rediscovered his daughter and is now squatting next to the kid, trying to reason with her, before giving up the fight and disappearing into the caravan to procure the lolly.

'And Eli, could you please put on some damn clothes. This isn't fucking Ibiza.'

Eli looks at me, though I cannot see her eyes behind the dark sunglasses she is wearing, and says, 'If we took a holiday, aha, oh yeah, took some time to celebrate, just one day out of life, it would be, it would be so nice.'

'Grow up,' I say, as she flops back down and covers her head with the top she could be wearing.

I fall asleep and dream of nothing.

When I open my eyes again it is cooler and the light has changed from golden to deep orange. The shadows are long and there are a few barbecues going in the vicinity. Ringlets of smoke reach for the sky.

'Here,' Eli says, and shoves a plastic goblet in my hand.

She is now wearing jeans and a man's flannel shirt, her hair is up in a loose bunch and her sunglasses are reflecting back my own groggy face.

I wonder, briefly, whose shirt she is wearing.

When I made a pass at her, years ago, she told me that I was too good for her. She leaned into my arms, her hair smelling of cigarette smoke and candyfloss, and she begged me not to want her in that way.

'How should I want you?' I asked.

'Like this,' she said, taking my hand and squeezing it, 'like this ...' leaning back and smiling at me like a child, utterly trusting and utterly selfish.

'What are you thinking?' Eli asks.

'I'm thinking that you are quite the little slut,' I reply and take a sip of my drink. Next to us, the father has fallen asleep in his chair and his daughter has disappeared.

'What do you think these people think when they see us?' I muse, partly to myself. 'You think they think we're screwing?'

Eli shrugs, and I can tell she is a few glasses ahead of me.

'You think they think we're weirdos?'

She snorts with laughter. 'These people are fucking weird.'

I look at her. 'You reckon? They seem like the core of normality to me.'

'Yeah, but normality is weird. Look at them, in their massive fuck-off tents and two point five children. You think any of them are actually happy?'

'Fuck Eli. Who's happy? Are you happy?'

She tilts her head to one side and purses her lips, considering. 'Sure I am. When I'm not depressed, I'm happy.'

'So you are happy, like, right now?'

'No, right now I'm fucking miserable. But if I were not then I would be happy.'

'So you wish you were back home? Going another round with what's his name?' It's a cheap thing to say, but I can't stand the eyes hidden behind her sunglasses, watching me as if I were made of stone or nothing at all. I can't fucking stand it.

'Hey,' she says, 'hey, don't do that. I'm never going back to that. Not ever.'

I might even believe her, if this weren't the fourth time she and what's-his-name had broken up. The first three times she came and stayed at my flat, got wasted and showed me her bruises. I asked her if she enjoyed getting hurt.

'I like that he can make me feel. Pain is feeling,' she had told me.

'Pain is feeling, like a fucking tornado is weather,' I had replied, not looking at her.

We both know this game, she would go back to him, and I would take her in when the shit hit the fan yet again. She would get drunk and saunter around my living room, a glorious mess, laughing and crying and undoing the buttons of her shirt to show me where it hurts. I'd touch her bruises – press the marbled heart of mauve and purple. Press it just a little bit too hard.

Something buzzes close to my face and I swat it aside, while Eli drains her goblet and puts it carefully down on the blanket next to her.

'You are a little fool,' I say, and she seems uncertain for a moment. Her hand trembles as she reaches for the empty goblet, takes a sip of nothing, and throws it to the ground.

'Maybe. But I know who matters. I know who cares about me, really cares.'

'Do you, really? And what does it matter?'

Eli removes her sunglasses and looks at me. The space between us catches fire, and I suddenly, violently, want to take her face between my hands and say to her *you stupid girl, you lovely, stupid, stupid girl*.

That's when we hear it: the scream. It is abrupt, jarring, and for a moment it does not seem human.

Around us people are looking about, startled, and the large guy sits up in his chair. Eli is on her feet before me, before anyone else, sprinting towards a grove of trees beyond the campsite, and I get up to follow her.

As I get closer I see a group of kids standing beneath the trees and I think, though I don't believe it, that they must be messing about.

Eli stops. She looks over her shoulder at me, her face smooth with fear.

At the bottom of one of the trees, sitting amongst the debris of dried leaves and twigs, is the little girl who was howling only a few hours ago. Her face is covered in blood, her blonde hair blackened and sleeked to one side of her skull.

She is silent.

Her eyes dart around at the children who are screaming next to her.

Eli kneels down next to the child and speaks, but the girl just stares ahead, her face ashen beneath the streaks of red, her eyes now fluttering wildly.

Heavy footsteps approach from the campsite, and I see the girl's father running towards us. His face changes when he sees her. It seems to melt into a terrible grimace as he keeps saying, over and over again, 'Oh my god, oh my god, oh my god.'

He shoves his way through the crowd that has gathered and gently scoops up the child in his arms and carries her off, while the rest of us stay behind in shocked silence.

Eli gets up from the ground and comes to me, and I put my arm around her. I hear the patter on the leaves above, feel a drop on my face.

The sky darkens as the rain begins to fall.

We're not waiting anymore.

The Returning

Playing Dead

NADINE BROWNE

Contents

Strange Fruit

Three hours from the West Australian border she starts losing it about the fruit in the car.

'Settle down,' I say. 'They're not gonna run out holding guns to our heads if we've got a few oranges in the car.'

'Well!' She turns to face me, one hand on the steering wheel. '*I* don't want to be paying the two thousand dollar *fine*!' With her free hand she reaches onto the back seat and whisks a bunch of bananas out the driver's side window.

'I was gonna eat those,' I say, but it's the third or fourth time she has mentioned fruit and she is beyond listening. The windows are down, the Dolly Parton CD is turned up and we are flying along the eastern plain of the Nullarbor.

And what will this desert do with such strange fruit? Animals might die; the entire precarious ecosystem that surrounds us may well turn on its head. She pulls out another cigarette, lights it, and aims the car down the very centre of the Eyre Highway. Without her noticing I lean back to get a glimpse of the speedometer. It is well past the 120 mark. Her head quivers slightly and she moves her jaw like she's grinding her teeth.

The banana incident is nothing. Only the day before she had threatened to leave me on the shore in Ceduna. I had attempted to go for a swim, not such a stupid idea considering it was February and the car had no air-conditioning. As I walked to the shore, she yelled out: 'There's sharks in that water. *Your* funeral.' I could see her sitting in the driver's seat, poking at the car stereo buttons. 'Oh yeah,' she yelled out, 'and don't expect us to make it back to Perth for Christmas lunch, either.'

Funny, her saying that. Back in Melbourne she said

she never wanted to go near Perth again. How any sane person could live there was a mystery to her; just one endless suburb of rednecks, in her opinion. It was time to move on, she said, and with that she went and spent her last three hundred dollars on a lime-green leather jacket and disappeared for two days. I traipsed across Melbourne looking for her, spurred on by a vague sense of duty that came with twenty years of friendship. I looked for her at the houses of various acquaintances and fellow West Australians in exile. When I did find her she was asleep on a couch in Brunswick. It was three p.m. on a Saturday and we were already two days behind schedule.

Adelaide onwards it hadn't been easy. I did most of the driving and she refused to answer simple questions like: 'Would you mind passing me the map book?' Or, when I asked, 'Did you see what that sign said?' she snapped, 'How the *fuck* should I know?'

Every CD I put on was either too mainstream, too happy or it was 'foreign shit'. We argued about the past, about the Bible, about whose mother was more depressed and whether it was better to have an alive father or one who was dead. But it wasn't long before I realised it was futile talking to her. I shut up; it was too hot to argue. She looked at me, her mouth turned down in disgust, and I evaded her gaze the way I'd seen people avoid drunken Aboriginals at the shopping centre. I looked everywhere but at her.

Perhaps, I think as we drive across the scrubby plain,

this is what happens to children whose parents teach them that society is something from which to separate themselves. Perhaps they grow up angry and hate everyone. As if reading my mind she says, 'You know what your problem is? *You're* stuck in the past, you can't get over it. *You're* fuckin' obsessed with it.'

I ponder this for a while, looking out to endless silver saltbush and the mysterious red desert tracks which trail off toward the faded blue sky. Finally I say, 'Well, I think it might have had some, you know, *influence* on our lives.'

'Bullshit! *That* is bullshit. I liked growing up there. In fact, I wish I was back there right now!'

'Great,' I say. 'Good for you.'

She sleeps a lot. It's a kind of tense, knotted-up sleep which she wakes from with a shiver and then squints with revulsion at the road in front. 'I hate driving,' she says, waking up as we leave Yalata. 'My whole childhood was just one long drive after another.' She puffs on another Dunhill Blue. 'Always off with Dad, building some church in the desert, for some boongs who couldn't give two shits about Jesus. Why the fuck you'd want to drive thousands of k's across the country?'

It wasn't like I'd forced her to come. In fact, it was she who had called me from Perth at two a.m. one morning, begging to stay with me in Melbourne. 'I need to get out of here,' she'd said. 'I can no longer remain here.' She used that overly formal way of speaking, which told me she was either high or drunk or both. 'It's just not a conducive environment to my mental and spiritual wellbeing,' she'd said. I hadn't talked to her for months. I explained that I was packing up, heading back home, it wasn't a good time.

We stop at the Nullarbor Roadhouse and it is here that

I see the familiar red and white of the WA Freightlines truck. It is the very same truck that has been tailgating and intermittently overtaking us since Adelaide. Entering the roadhouse, I pass what can only be the driver: shorts, thongs, an inordinate amount of body hair.

While she is pacing up and down out the front of the roadhouse, this truck driver, in a moment of acute folly, wolf-whistles at her.

'You fuckin' prick!' she screams, throwing a fist in the truck driver's direction. 'You can *fuck off*!' Luckily, at this exact moment, I am walking out of the roadhouse into the hot wind and blinding light with my seven-dollar Cornetto. I manage to grab her arm as she lunges for his faded blue singlet. Her screaming disturbs the dusk silence that lies all around, from the veranda of the roadhouse to the furthest horizon. She lunges at the truck driver again, almost knocking me to the ground.

I realise, there is something wrong. As I try to pull her back I feel her muscles and cartilage pulsating under my hands. It is the shock of touching her cold, clammy skin that gets my attention; it's a hot day, at least thirty-five degrees. Her anger is not the hot rage of a young, angry woman, but the cold, septic anger of someone sick and desperate. I look at her far too skinny frame, the greyness around her eyes, the glistening cut of her muscles, formed as if they belonged to someone much older than twenty-three.

Back in the car I polish off what may have been the most expensive ice-cream in Australia. She sits in the passenger seat, filling the car with obscenities and cigarette smoke. 'They should all have their dicks cut off,' she announces and then, almost abruptly, she falls asleep and stays that way for a good few hours. I keep to the 110 speed limit and rummage around the car in search of a CD I haven't heard seventeen times.

The car, even with all the windows down, reeks of cigarettes, a pack a day no less. At every roadhouse I had bought a packet, sometimes two. I calculate: thirteen dollars times three, no four, what's that? Fifty-two dollars, *that's fifty-two dollars* – isn't like I'm going to see that money again. But if she is like this with cigarettes, I don't want to see what she's like without them. Even I have started smoking, which isn't helping the situation. I pick up a CD from under her feet, *The Sounds of Spain*. It is badly scratched but still plays and I try to occupy myself with the sounds of flamenco music. Of course, trying to distract yourself from emotional angst with a musical version of it doesn't work all that well. As I listen to the wailing and the stomping of feet a dark mood swirls over me, as wide and full as a flamenco skirt.

I have crossed the plain several times but I cannot remember, or even imagine, how it ends. It seems it will go on forever and I fantasise, while meditating on the beat of the dotted white line, that Perth must be some kind of special, secret place to be on the other side of this. Only some place that was truly great could be this hard to get to. That I still fill my mind with such ideas of a Promised Land, that I still consider suffering as being worthwhile, is disappointing. I know in reality I will feel let down. I know that Perth, like always, will seem like just another rest stop along the way to a more proper, more well-rounded place.

When we finally make it to the border, the woman at the gate has on more foundation than her face can actually contain. It is all running off down her neck on account of the heat and her eyelashes look like some sort of modern outdoor verandas with black shade cloth over them. My travelling companion tells the lady that she looks nice. She calls the lady 'honey' in that fake, high-pitched voice she uses when she wants people to think she's from some place where chai lattes and baked cheesecake are served. When the lady asks us to pop the boot she jokes that there is nothing to see but 'sixteen ounces of coke'.

'Oh,' she says, with such a dramatic flourish that the lady raises her heavily pencilled eyebrows, 'but I'd never dream of bringing *fruit* into our beloved state.' I stare on, daunted, after three days in the car, by the exhausting complexities of human interaction.

Miraculously, we are granted entry into our home state. The lady and a thin, leathery man are mainly concerned with fruit, not our emotional wellbeing. They say if we have any fruit we should put it in the tray, and they both point to it. They say it twice. They say, 'Dried fruit, stone fruit, honey or nuts.' The lady's eyes dart between the two of us as her foundation continues its escape down her cheeks and toward the gold chains around her neck. I look out to the desert on either side of us, out on the red infertile earth, the low-lying orange sun, the straight, grey road ahead, and I think how fruit should be the furthest thing from my mind.

'*Well*, I thought she did look nice,' she says when we are back in the car. 'At least she made an *effort*. I mean, it can't be *easy* in this dump, waking up every morning making a fucking *effort*!' She spits out the words like I'm the one that's holding society back, as if I'm the enemy of anyone in the world who has ever made an effort.

At Eucla, I pull up in front of the giant whale and get out to fill the car. She sits with the door open and her feet on the ground. She has that same faraway look that she had when I found her on the couch in Brunswick, it's as if she's just arrived in a dream, here on the side of the Eyre Highway. She asks if she can borrow some money and I hand her a fifty-dollar note, telling her to pay for the petrol as well.

I stand in front of the ridiculous Eucla whale and I remember a long time ago, at another equally desolate roadhouse. The two of us were heading to a Christian mission near Kununurra. Amos, the pastor's son, was with us. It was the middle of the night and the trip had taken more hours than our teenage minds could comprehend. At this one particular roadhouse, she had wanted to buy a Guns N' Roses tape. We looked at the tape for a long time, trying to interpret some iniquitous meaning on the cover, some subtle, devious message from Satan himself. Soon Amos came and told us to get back in the truck. He was on the lookout for just such worldly distractions.

I remember that night, how she did a half-skip back to the truck and waved to some Aboriginal boys standing in the darkness nearby. She had seemed so excited about even the possibility that one day we would be able to buy that tape, and listen to it, and how great it would be. Even then I remember thinking how bold and happy she had looked. That night it was the other side of midnight, we were sixteen and it was the first time we had been allowed to leave the community without our parents.

Amos had not been impressed. He went on for a while about the path of wrongdoing being wide, how its gates were always open. 'Rock music is one of Satan's favourite lures,' he said. 'It all seems cool and fun until you realise Satan's got hold of your life, oh he's got a good strong hold on it then,' and with his hands still resting on the steering wheel, he curled his fingers around as if he were throttling something. She and I took turns sitting in the window seat and, sometime during the night, while I had my arm out, the desert air went from warm to cold so suddenly that I drew back my arm in fear. I wanted to tell her, but when I turned she was looking intently into the blackness, and she whispered, 'I haven't seen any lights so far, not one.'

There are parts of Western Australia where you forget that the world is actually filled with billions of people. You think that the entire world should know you, because your entire world does. They know your mother, your father; they know your kitchen table, the size of your feet and how your voice sounds when you are frightened. You can't imagine a world where people don't. The world that she and I came from was like that, and while the outside was exciting and full of new and compelling things, it was also full of disappointment.

I stand by the Eucla whale for a long time, just me and the whale and that sky. I think about how Eucla always makes me feel small, like I've been shrunk in the wash. I look up from the car park and stars are already appearing in half the sky, the other half is still filled with the sun, about to go down over those snow-white dunes to the south.

Overseas, I once met a man who had never seen a shooting star. He wasn't exactly a young man. I wanted to tell him that Eucla means 'bright star' in the local Aboriginal language. I wanted to tell him that in Eucla the sky is so big it makes you feel you're nothing at all. I wanted to explain to him how the night skies in Eucla are filled with more shooting stars than you can count. But how do you start to tell someone about Eucla, when you're both in some cold, claustrophobic place like Cardiff, or Manchester, or wherever I was.

With the money, she had bought almost everything in the bain-marie: two Chiko rolls, a sausage roll, a pie and hot chips. I drive on towards Balladonia while she sits stuffing her face. The sun now a red glow on the horizon, I watch as the grey plain to the right side of the road shifts. The entire plain begins to hop, glide and bound at the side of the car, in front of the car and then all over the road, red and grey, big and small, the landscape teems with them. I slow to sixty and hold down the horn. Even then I have to ride the brake to avoid hitting them, a few still careening into the side of the car as they make their irrational escape to the other side of the road.

At Balladonia the eight official residents of the place sit around a large bonfire. They are full of Christmas cheer and a few cartons of Emu Draft. 'Geez, you girls must have seen some roos,' one of them says. We sit a while and eat the lamb chops they offer, drink the beers they hand us. After an hour or so we announce that we should get moving. 'Perth isn't getting any closer,' we say. They say we are crazy. We don't disagree.

I have developed the same itch as her, scratching at my arms furiously with one hand on the steering wheel. My head churns over and over with its circular, nagging chatter – the few cans of Emu Draft make it churn faster. A feral cat the size of a blue heeler appears on the dark roadside, the bone-white trunks of the ghost gums are illuminated by our lights.

'So,' I say, feeling uncomfortable with the unfamiliar sound of my own voice, 'why'd you have to get out of Perth?'

She sighs and props her arm on the windowsill. Up ahead, small, faded signs, some handwritten, appear in the headlights and point to mines or drilling operations off the road. 'I don't know,' she sighs, 'I was staying at the Duxton with Ben, we were on a bender, like for three or four days.' Ben had grown up with us, his parents also raging born-again Christians. 'I went to sleep, left a tap on after he'd gone. It flooded the whole penthouse.' She scratches her arm, then tucks her hair behind her ear. 'Ben says I owe eight grand in damages, says it was my fault.'

I doubt this is the real reason. Ben, since growing up, had gone from a quiet, sulky, fat kid to becoming a fully patched member of the Coffin Cheaters. On a big weekend he could spend eight grand on drinks alone. I don't say anything. I take another of her cigarettes and keep driving.

'Perth is not where I wanna be right now,' she says, 'but, I dunno, where is there? I mean, where is there to get to?'

I ash the cigarette out the slit of the open window, mumble that I don't know, how should I know? Nobody knows. What I want to say is that I've also been moving. What I want to say is, I don't see where there is to get to, either. When you spend half your life waiting for Jesus to return, maybe this is just what happens after, maybe this is what you're left with.

At close to one a.m. I stop to get a coffee and use the toilets at Norseman Roadhouse. When I come back to the car she is gone; the cigarettes and her bag are gone, too. There is no movement in the car park, the street in front is quiet, only a gentle breeze moves the leaves on the trees. A streetlight shines on the highway out the front of the roadhouse. It's a harsh, white triangle of light, so bright against the blackness it seems like it could be picked up and moved elsewhere. I imagine her running under the light with her bag over her shoulder, running into the darkness somewhere, anywhere. As if I was the enemy.

The Jerry Can

When I saw Melita walking across the street with a jerry can, I took note. It was not so much the jerry can that intrigued me, it was her leaving her house. I'd never actually seen her in the full light of day and her obesity was astounding. Her pink pyjama top came halfway down her thighs, exposing heavy clouds of white flesh.

I'd just gotten out of bed. I was usually woken by the kids coming home from school and the reason I peeked out the venetians in the first place was because I could hear one of them screaming. It was Melita's eight-year-old Justin from behind the screen door. 'Mum, Mum,' he wailed, 'come back!' I could see his fingers coming through the large rips in the flyscreen of their security door.

I watched as Melita's body shuddered with each aftershock of her bare feet hitting the ground. The jerry can swung by her side. Just putting one foot in front of the other seemed like a great act of defiance. I stood in awe at my bedroom window and a part of me thought: if she can do it, I can too.

A moment later she disappeared from view, into the front yard of the house next door to mine. 'Muuuum!' The kid at the flyscreen pushed the sound out from the bottom of his throat; it had that terrorised, distressed quality, which makes you really feel another's pain. *Settle down, kid,* I thought, *she's just crossing the street.* I waited, standing mesmerised and half-blinded by the harsh white light coming through the gap in the blinds. The kid's wailing filled the whole street, echoing off the asphalt. I waited, and after a few moments I heard her shout, 'It's all right, Jay, I'm just here.' Her voice was impatient as she puffed her way back across the street, past a couple of discarded shopping trolleys. Her dimpled skin shimmering in the sunlight, she made her way up her short, toy-strewn driveway and then back through the front door of her house.

About an hour later, after taking my assortment of pills, I went outside to water the trees. Most days this is the only time I leave the house. I put my sunglasses on and looked over at Melita's house. Directly across from mine, her house had the unkempt and unloved finish shared with many of the welfare houses in the area, the once bright orange of the rendered front wall now a faded dusty pink. Many of the squat decorative pickets of the front fence were missing and wild oats grew high between the fence and the footpath. There was no sign of Melita.

I watered the six lemon trees I'd grafted, then moved on to all my other assortments of trees: pin oaks, silky oaks, olive, avocado and fig. All in pots, they take up my entire backyard and most of the front yard, too.

Soon enough Melita's kids came out. She's got four kids, all under eleven. They're all lithe and thin and wispy, like they could be blown away in a gust of wind; all blond with tanned little bodies. The twins went running off down the street, then Justin ran towards my house. They always run; everywhere they go, they're running.

He jumped over the knee-high brick fence and said, 'Can I help water?' I handed him the hose, then busied myself with some weeding.

'Will these trees grow big like that one?' Justin pointed to the cape lilac, 'if I keep watering them?'

'They should do.'

'What do you keep all these trees in pots for?' he asked.

'I like trees,' I said.

Justin looks at me with wonder, like he's never heard of anyone liking trees before, it's never crossed his mind.

'You must like 'em heaps.'

For some reason, even though he's just a little kid, I felt a hotness at the top of my ears, and light-headed from holding my breath. I looked back down at the ground, concentrating on the few stubborn weeds left.

'But what are you gonna do with them all?'

'I don't know,' I said, chewing my bottom lip. What I didn't tell him was that the trees are what I used to fill my nights with, that the trees were the reason I got into trouble, the reason I had to start seeing Georgina, the psychiatrist.

'Did your mum run out of petrol before?' I asked.

'No.' He sounded defensive. 'She just needed to tell those people something, Akira's mum and dad. My mum hates Akira's mum and dad.'

'Why?'

'They're bad.' He shrugged. 'They take drugs.'

At that moment Akira came riding her bike down the sidewalk.

'What are you starin' at?' she shouted to Justin.

'Your mum 'n' dad are gonna go to jail coz they takes drugs.'

'Shut up, Justin.' Akira stopped her bike at the fence, one foot on the ground anchoring her to the spot. 'They don't even take drugs anymore.' She wore a pink one-piece that roped around her neck and was tight on her tubby young body.

'My mum said they do.'

'Well your mum's a fat cow and she only eats McDonald's which is funny coz her second name is McDonald!' Akira threw her bike down and hoisted herself up on the brick wall. I looked up at her from where I crouched, in front of the garden bed. Despite her small chubby limbs and pink one-piece she looked imposing.

'What are youse doing anyway?' she said, looking down on us.

'War-terin',' Justin said proudly.

'Can I do some?'

'No. I'm only allowed.'

'She can have a turn,' I said.

She jumped down from the wall and ran across the yard to where the end of the hose was. She yanked it off Justin, then tucked her brown unbrushed hair behind one of her ears and concentrated on the line of heavy water shooting towards the big avocado tree.

'Anyway, Justin, my mum says that your mum goes out and hocks stuff while you're at school. That's why she never has any money; she's always at the hock shop hocking things to buy junk food. She looooves junk food.'

'Hey,' I said. 'You shouldn't talk about people like that. It's not nice.' I hated the sound of me telling them off. I was never sure how to communicate with children, always frightened of inadvertently dabbing them with the poison that had afflicted me my whole life.

'She doesn't even hock stuff anymore, Akira,' Justin explained. 'She only did it coz we had no money.'

That night, I lay awake thinking about Melita and her kids. I thought I should give them a tree each to grow themselves. The vision of her crossing the street stayed in my mind, she seemed so vulnerable and exposed. How did she keep up with those kids when she could hardly move? I wondered. Then I thought I'd be sure to tell Georgina my psychiatrist all this on Friday. She'd be happy. She was always telling me I needed to make friends, become more involved in my community. I also needed to realise, Georgina said, that I had something to offer. But I didn't ever think that was the problem; it's just what I had to give, nobody wanted.

What I hadn't realised was that staying up all night 'doing things' and obsessing over the trees was the beginning of my mania. I had to watch for signs, keep vigilant, adhere to an achievable routine – and that took a lot of energy.

At about three a.m. I smelt smoke. I put down the book I was reading, concentrating on the smell, and quickly realised that it was all around me. The room had filled with it. As I listened I could hear people yelling outside. I tiptoed on the floorboards to the front door and before I'd opened it the orange light was already coming through the glass. I stepped out and heard the roar, and, running out onto my front veranda, I saw flames galloping upwards, round and fierce, reaching towards the black night sky. I couldn't look away. The house next door, Akira's house, was completely swallowed by fire. It cracked and popped and banged but the sound was muted by its all-encompassing roar. Heat was coming from it and I felt exposed in my synthetic nightie.

I didn't know what I should do. Then someone yelled at me from the street: 'You gotta hose? Where's your hose, love?' It was the old woman on the other side of me. She walked through my front gate and straight up to the corner of my house where the hose lay neatly in a circle. Before I got to the tap she was turning it on. 'You gotta watch out for the embers, just keep water on that side.' She dragged the hose around to the far side of my house and started spraying water on it.

'What happened?' I asked.

'Who knows? I just come out to see what all the noise was about, 'n' there it was, in full force.' I'd never seen the old lady up close before. From a distance she looked younger, but now I could see she only had a few yellow teeth and the deep crevices in her face were highlighted by the orange glow of the fire. 'Just keep the water on,' she instructed, handing me the hose and then walking away. I squinted into the heat of the fire and just when I thought the flames couldn't get any stronger an explosion erupted at the back of the burning house. Red embers shot into the sky like fireworks. Shouts came from the street where a crowd of people had gathered. Akira's mum was there, I could just make her out, silhouetted under the streetlight. She was thrashing about, screaming, held back by two men from the street.

The sirens got louder until two red trucks, a big and a small one, pulled up in the front yard of the house. The firemen unravelled hoses and shot water at the base of the flames. Within a few minutes it was all out and the black flatness of where the house had been was remarkably quiet. The fire trucks remained at the front. The old woman left the crowd and came towards me again. I couldn't be sure, but it looked like her face was wet.

'The girl, Akira, she was inside.'

'Inside what?' I asked.

'She, she got left in there.' She pointed to what remained of the house next door. 'Poor sweet little baby.' She shook her head, and I noticed the wrinkles under her chin quiver a little.

I looked over at the still smoking, collapsed frame of

the house. The tin roof was now at ground level. I kept repeating the old woman's words in my head: 'She got left in there, got left in *there*.' But my brain was slow and old and wouldn't catch up.

'But I just saw her this afternoon,' I said, looking at the old lady. She shrugged, and her eyes, I could see now, were red. Her face looked like all the air had been let out of it.

The police said that the fire had been started by the meth lab. I didn't know what a meth lab was and the two officers who came to my house had to explain it all to me. I kept wanting to talk about the girl, like if I built enough of a picture of her, she could be restored, the police would find her, like she was a missing person. They said the father had died too, trying to save her. They said if I remembered anything else, to call them. I put their card on the fridge. I'd forgotten all about Melita and the jerry can.

A few weeks later I was sitting in the waiting room of Georgina's office going through what I would tell her in my head when my ear caught the receptionist on the phone. 'Hello, Melita?' she said. 'Hello. It's Rachel from Morrison House Clinic. Is that Melita McDonald?'

I sat still and tense, concentrating on the receptionist's voice. 'Are you aware that you missed your appointment with Dr Greenburg this morning?'

That's when I remembered the jerry can. I hadn't seen her since that morning.

'Well, would you like to reschedule?' the receptionist was asking. 'What about Friday?'

Then I heard Georgina's voice calling my name. I got up and went into her office.

'How have you been?' She smiled and sat down in the chair across from me.

'Okay. I guess I've been okay.'

Georgina's office is a mixture of sophisticated coppery figurines – abstract humans and swans – and two-dollar store knick-knacks.

'And since the fire?' she asked. 'Have you talked to your neighbours at all?'

'I talked to the old woman, well she talks to me; she said she knew they were making drugs. She'd told the police, been telling them for a long time, everyone in the street had.'

Georgina pursed her lips in some show of empathy, I suppose. She was middle-aged, plump and had short grey hair. I thought she might have been a lesbian, because on the phone she sounded like a man and she always wore pants.

'I didn't know, though,' I said, 'I didn't know they were drug dealers.' My eyes moved across the mantelpiece to a doll dressed in a suit and tie. 'I keep thinking about that little girl, the day she came to my house; it was the afternoon before the fire.' My eyes focused on the doll. I held my face very still so I wouldn't show any emotion. 'I liked her. Akira. She was, I don't know, tough. I think the word you would use is … resilient.' I picked at the corner of the armrest. 'I'm not like that. I've got no resilience. I'm like the wrong tree planted in the wrong spot at the wrong time.'

'Well, you've had a pretty traumatic life, you didn't get to build up a lot of resilience.' Georgina always likes to make excuses for me, she's quite good at it.

'She used to come and talk to me when I watered and she was always climbing the trees, she loved to climb everything, she just couldn't stop moving.' I stared hard at the ceramic feet of the doll and let out a big sigh. I got sick of talking pretty quick around Georgina.

'I told you about the obese woman across the road and her kids?' I said.

'Yes, you said you wanted to, possibly, reach out to them?'

'Well, she comes here.' I watched Georgina's face for a reaction. She only furrowed her eyebrows slightly.

'And I didn't tell you about the jerry can.'

'Jerry can?' Georgina frowned.

'I saw her. Melita. The morning of the fire, she walked over to that house with a jerry can.'

There was silence and I felt something around my jaw relax like it was a relief to say it out loud.

But Georgina never misses a beat. She said, 'Well, you need to tell the police about that. That's all you need to do, tell the police.' And then of course she came back to the subject we always ended up at: trees.

'What about the tree planting and your insomnia?' she asked. 'How have you been handling that?'

'I haven't been planting any *trees*. I've been distracting myself,' I said, 'reading, watching the documentaries I got from the DVD store.'

'Great. And the medication?'

'All going fine.' I nodded.

'I'm pleased to hear it. You know there are a lot of good organisations you can be part of that plant trees legally. They help farmers and assist with reforestation. It's something you could think about being part of.'

I tried to look interested. The thing about the trees is, I planted them all over the neighbourhood and all the surrounding suburbs. When the council chopped them down, I planted three more for every one they got rid of. That was what I got arrested for. The judge said I was a menace to public property; I had caused the taxpayer thousands of dollars in tree removal. They said it was no better than graffiti what I was doing, and as a mature-aged woman I should know better. I said I couldn't help it, it was a compulsion. That's when they ordered me to see a psychiatrist.

I couldn't sleep that night after I'd seen Georgina. I got up and looked at the card the police left me on the fridge. I should call them, I thought, tell them what I saw. But then I thought about what might happen to Melita, and what would happen to her kids. The thing about Melita was, like me, she never had visitors. The only car I'd seen at her house was a welfare car. Welfare visited a lot of the houses around here. I'd come to recognise their same model car, the same coloured folders, the same kind of harried middle-aged women they hired, who always travelled in pairs. I paced up and down the hallway. I took a long hot bath to try to make myself tired. Maybe Melita knew they were making drugs in the house, I thought, but that didn't make what she'd done any better.

I went for a long walk in the middle of the night. I walked fast, and even tried running, although my hip pain wouldn't allow too much of that. I walked for hours, all through the outer suburbs. Mostly it was quiet, sometimes I heard shouts and screams, raucous laughter. I looked through windows when there was a light on. I wondered what people were dreaming of behind dark, curtained windows. It seemed to me that the outer suburbs sat on the edge of a cliff that was dropping away and everyone was terrified of falling into the abyss. As I walked I could feel their terror.

I walked further and further out, beyond my own suburb and everywhere I went my mind kept seeing places to plant a tree. No matter how hard I tried to think of other things, every roundabout, every barren verge, every island in the road, what they all needed, more than anything, was trees.

Two nights later I sat up in bed and decided the feeling I'd been having for the past three weeks, ever since the house fire, could no longer be ignored. I decided, despite what Georgina told me, that once in a while you have to act on your feelings, otherwise you may as well be dead. I got out of bed and got dressed.

The feeling was a type of restlessness, but it was also something my body wanted to rid itself of, like when you see children with too much energy, they need to expel it. I realised, despite the antidepressants, the sleeping pills and the therapy, I still had nothing against it.

I grabbed a shopping trolley off the sidewalk and filled it with my biggest trees; I piled them high, as many as I could balance on top of one another. I got the shovel, I got some compost. I piled it all up, and then I started off down the street.

I pushed the trolley along backstreets, through the industrial area, under bypasses and down the highway until I came to the sandy, inconsequential island I had in mind. I took a cedar wattle out from the jam-packed trolley. I put the shovel into the ground and pressed hard on it with my foot. I listened to the satisfying sound of the shovel going through the earth. That first moment, as the shovel cuts into the soil, it feels like I'm really part of something – something so big I couldn't even try to contain it in my mind. It was like, for once, I was not hovering about like a nervous insect banging against glass. Instead, my feet were firmly on the ground.

The digging and planting went well into the night. Tree after tree after tree, until the trolley was empty. All my joints seemed to cry out, but it was a good type of pain, the pain of moving forward, the pain of progress, the pain of giving. I started to walk home. I got to my street with my shovel resting on my shoulder. A yellow hue was already coming up in the east.

As I came to Melita's house, I noticed the lights were on and when I got closer I could see her massive figure standing in the doorway. She was looking out her front door to the block across the road where the house used to be. They had cleaned it up, taken away every remnant of the house. It looked like it had always been just another vacant block.

I stood in her driveway and faced her in the doorway. The street and the whole suburb was so quiet at that time, I didn't need to talk very loud. In a strong whisper, I said, 'I saw you, you know, with the jerry can.'

The screen door opened and she heaved her giant mass out towards me.

'I didn't mean for it to happen.' Her voice sounded high and thin, like a young girl's.

'But I saw you,' I said.

'I doused the petrol around, and I was gonna light it up, but I changed my mind. I couldn't do it.' She let out a pent-up sigh, she had that glassy panic in her eye that I sometimes see in the mirror and I could tell she had been up all night thinking about it. 'I couldn't do it with kids in the house,' she said.

I wanted to say something mean, something to make her realise what she'd done, but I couldn't think of anything. I felt tired now and all I could wonder about was if the little girl had died in her sleep or if she'd woken up.

'I haven't stopped thinking about her, you know. Akira.' Melita took a few steps towards me. I tried to look at her face, but my eyesight wasn't very good these days and I was having trouble adjusting to the morning light.

'But why did you do it?'

'I didn't want a meth lab around here, around my kids.' She shook her head and looked at the ground. She was higher than me on the driveway, which sloped up to her door. 'If you tell the cops I'll lose my kids. I know I probably deserve to, but those kids are all I've got.' I looked down at her iridescent white feet on the sandy driveway paving, then I turned and started walking across the road to my house.

*⁣**

I'd been thinking about it for a while; what kind of tree would Akira be? Something hardy and native, something statuesque and bold. The next day, after the kids came home from school, I told them we would plant a tree on the verge out the front of the vacant block next door. I went around to all the neighbours and told them I was planting a tree for Akira. We all took turns digging a big hole. I worked the silky oak out of its pot. Its white exposed roots looked fragile and delicate. I passed the tree to Justin and the twins and they dropped it in the hole. All of us pushed the dirt around it with our hands. We all stood looking at it for a while, the old lady from next door and her grandsons, Melita and the kids, the Aboriginal family that lived next to her, the man from the corner. It was the perfect spot for it. Even though it had only just been planted, it looked right; strong and robust. A welling up started in my chest as I watched the cool, silvery leaves shining in the afternoon sun.

Clean

Summer remembered the exact point at which it had all started. It was a Monday afternoon at Francine's house, she grabbed a chair at the kitchen table. Toys and crayons and dirty plates were scattered all over. A large puddle of blue sticky liquid had gone dry on the floor nearby. In front of her Francine put her hand to her chest and breathed out hard. 'The baby is in your bag,' she said quickly, though she couldn't see Summer's bag or the baby. Summer got up and walked around the kitchen bench to see the one-year-old behind the lounge; the contents of the bag were all over the floor and he had a tampon in his mouth. Summer remembered looking around and thinking it was like someone had picked up the whole house and shaken it. She could tell by the way Francine sat with her eyes fixed on the edge of the kitchen bench that she had something to say. Summer sat back down at the kitchen table and Francine moved a pot of tea towards her. 'Well, Pete's leaving me,' she said. 'He's found a place.'

'So it's final?' Summer raised her eyebrows. Pete had threatened to leave before but she didn't think he would actually go through with it.

'And before you say anything,' Francine raised her voice above the children who were jumping off the back of the couch onto the lounge-room floor, 'I'm keeping the house, I'll take on more cleaning.'

'You can't take on more with the kids.'

Francine shrugged and Summer watched her chin dimple and her lips purse hard across her face. The tears she was trying to keep down came up and filled her eyes. Summer waited for them to drop but they didn't, it was like her face sucked them right back up from where they'd come.

'Hey,' Summer whispered. She put her hand on Francine's forearm. She wanted to say whatever it was you said in these situations, but panic stopped her. Four kids? she thought, and one with autism; a massive mortgage, no family support? Her brain raced in search for something positive to say. Then she remembered what her Narcotics Anonymous sponsor had said to her a few years back. 'Sometimes you just have to feel like complete and utter crap, and nothing I say is going to make it any better.'

She kept her hand on Francine's forearm and looked out the window at the sharp lines of the neighbouring fence. They were in the cardboard cut-out land of the new developments. Sitting at the kitchen table, Summer envisioned the mortgage belt around them as the leather belt of an obese old man, he loosened a few notches and the bulldozers cleared more land. At that moment, all Summer could think was that underneath all of this used to be desert. Then she thought, how long can it go on like this?

Two weeks later they were at a cleaning job, scrubbing the grout in an ensuite bathroom in a house in Darling Ridge. A few years before they had started a cleaning business together, which, it turned out, had been a good move for two women with little education or employment prospects.

Francine was on her hands and knees scrubbing by the

sink and Summer was getting in between the toilet and the wall.

Francine said, 'You remember that house we used to clean in Seabourne, across from the beach? With the chandeliers and the pomeranian?'

'Yeah?' Summer said.

'Remember the box of money we found? And those Cartier watches?'

'Yeah, what about it?'

'Well, you know what it's like, some of these suburbs, during the day there's not a single person home for streets.' Francine scrubbed at the grout furiously.

'Double income no kids, that's what you need to live out there,' Summer added.

'And people are pretty lax with their home security.'

'Well, it's a good neighbourhood; I guess they think they don't need to worry.' Summer couldn't understand why she felt the need to act dumb because she knew exactly what Francine was getting at. But she let Francine talk; in fact, she felt a bubbling up in her stomach, headed towards her chest. It had always been Summer who'd done the crazy things, the things she couldn't get herself out of, she'd lived for that – for one illicit adventure after the next. Now it was like she was egging Francine on.

They were quiet for a while, only the sounds of hard bristles against the tiles between them. Every now and then they dipped their brushes in the ice-cream container of vinegar between them, and its tangy acidic bite filled the bathroom.

'Because I'm not moving out of my house,' Francine said as if the two things were connected.

'Well, maybe you won't have to.'

'Thing is,' Francine paused, 'Pete's redrawn off the

mortgage.'

Summer stopped scrubbing, sat up and looked over at her friend.

'About seventy grand he's whittled away.'

Summer looked back at the tiles in front of her, enraged. 'Jeez,' she hissed. She couldn't imagine what Pete had needed seventy grand for, he'd stacked warehouse shelves for thirteen years, he had no interests, no motivation, no ambition.

'What'd he spend it on?' she squinted at Francine.

Francine frowned, she had moved onto the tiles around the shower screen. 'Basically the mortgage is bigger than when we started.'

'Did you ask him, Francine? Did you ask him what he did with seventy grand?' Summer felt herself getting annoyed at her friend's lack of emotion.

'Course I did. He said *living expenses*.'

Summer shook her head and felt a drop of sweat come off her chin and land on the tiles underneath her.

'So anyway,' Francine went on, 'I'm sick to death of lying awake at night thinking how I'm gonna make these mortgage payments. And you know what I can't stop thinking about, you know what comes to my mind most nights?'

'What?'

'Those Louis Vuitton handbags she had.'

'Oh come on, Francine.'

'No, listen, that stuff was real, do you know how much they're worth? I do, I've looked it up on the internet – four thousand a pop! And the Cartier watches?' she snorted, 'my God, Summer, I nearly cried when I saw them. Remember I showed you? Remember all those crazy fuckin' diamond and pearl–encrusted watches? You remember.'

Summer remembered. She remembered that stab of awe that constricted her throat – or was it anger? She remembered catching a glimpse of herself in the dressing table mirror of the supersized walk-in robe and being revolted by her pockmarked, hard-edged face.

'Francine,' Summer whispered, 'don't even talk like this.' She got up from the floor and emptied the ice-cream container down the sink.

***

A few days later they were cleaning a house in Woodbridge. Summer was running water from the kitchen tap into the mop bucket.

'You could get your teeth fixed,' Francine said. They had only just arrived at the job and it was the first thing Francine had said to her. Summer almost choked on her own breath when she said that. She coughed.

'Well, you could. You could go to Bali and get your teeth done.'

Summer clenched her jaw and then ran her tongue over the shattered ridges and crevices of her teeth. She couldn't believe Francine would mention that now. Of course she was embarrassed about her teeth. Seven years of methamphetamine addiction had ravaged her mouth. She never gave a full smile, making sure to always cover her mouth with her top lip.

'Just don't, Francine,' she shook her head and snapped the kitchen tap closed, then hoisted the steaming bucket to the floor.

'Really, what have you got to lose, Summer?' Francine was pulling out vacuum cleaner attachments.

'We could end up in jail for a start, then what are you

gonna tell your kids? I mean, maybe life isn't as peachy as we thought it'd be back in high school, but it could be a lot worse.'

'Could be a lot better too.'

Summer rolled her eyes. She didn't want to hear any more about it. Really, she thought, she was finished with trying to grab hold of something bigger in her life. Mostly she was just trying to get through each day, moment by moment, baby steps, all of that, just like everyone else at her Narcotics Anonymous support group.

'Well, everywhere I look,' Francine continued, 'every house I go into, people are in a better financial situation than me. I mean, look around, Summer, you think these people are struggling?'

Summer looked out into the sunken lounge room, past the brand new leather settee and the Turkish rugs to the view of the river.

'You don't know that, Francine. Maybe they are struggling, maybe they just hide it really well.'

Francine laughed. 'Look, it's not like we're hurting anybody, everyone's insured and we see people doing way worse, like this guy on the telly that's ripped all the oldies off their life savings.' Summer had seen it on the news the night before too. The Ponzi guy.

'Please, Francine, this break-and-enter stuff, it's what drug addicts do, not a working mother of four. I mean, I've been there, it's a tangled web, it's one thing after another, one lie after another. I know where it ends up.' Summer plunged the mop head into the bucket.

'Just listen, just hear me out,' Francine was shouting, her voice echoed through the massive, sparsely decorated open-plan house. She pointed a feather duster in the air. 'A couple of grand is nearly three weeks in mortgage payments.' She thrust three fingers in front of her like she was explaining something to her hyperactive children. 'That puts me ahead, that means I don't have to move, and me and the kids don't have to live in a *shit* box, in a *shitty* neighbourhood and rely on welfare. It means I have some self-respect.' She gestured wildly with the feather duster, then tapped it on the kitchen bench to bring home her point. 'All I wanted was a nice family home, a safe place that actually feels like a home. And that house *is* my home.'

'It's just a house, Francine. Fuck, they're all just houses,' Summer waved her arm towards the lounge room. 'Maybe you'd like where you moved to, maybe something smaller would be better, we both know it'd be easier to clean.'

'Is it too much to ask?' Summer could hear the rage in Francine's voice and it frightened her. 'To want to stay in my own home? The home that I've worked so damn hard for?' Francine finally put the feather duster down on the bench then leant against it. 'Stability,' she announced, 'you know what that is? It's something we never had, our mothers couldn't rub two cents together, pushed from pillar to post, I don't want to repeat *that* kind of history around my kids.' She yanked at the cord of the vacuum cleaner, then plugged it into the nearby socket. 'Plus, I've got good memories in that house.'

Summer wanted to remind her she had bad memories too, but she didn't say anything. She wanted her to shut up. Her disintegrated teeth ground hard together in her mouth and she pushed her tongue against them.

'You know, all that cash was just sitting there, they probably wouldn't even miss it.' Francine was putting the wood floor attachment on the end of the vacuum.

'They probably don't live there anymore,' Summer said.

'They do, I drove past and saw that bitch getting out of

her Volvo. And I bet that lounge-room window still doesn't close properly.' Summer caught Francine's eye and blinked hard.

'This is crazy, Francine, totally crazy. They'd trace it back to us. I've already got a criminal record.'

***

At home, Summer threw herself on the couch in front of the television, like she did every night. Her whole body ached, joints swollen and hard. She watched *Renovation Rescue* with the sound off, then *Dream Homes by the Sea*, then she turned it over to *Extreme Home Makeover*. She looked around at the haphazard trappings of her one-bedroom unit with disgust. She was meant to call her Narcotics Anonymous sponsor but could not stop herself from staring into the muted TV screen.

Apparently she was depressed; her sponsor had told her it was normal to feel like this when giving up an addiction. Summer thought she might just be bored. She thought her forty-two years on the planet might have gone smoother if someone had thought to inform her that life was actually pretty mundane. Then she would have been ready for it. She would have accepted all the boring tedium thrown at her. She felt that she had always been waiting, in a state of extreme anticipation for something incredible to happen. That's why she had turned to drugs. Drugs made things incredible, for a while at least. Her mobile phone vibrated in her top pocket. It was her sponsor, Renae.

'Hi Renae.'

Renae asked how her day had been. She called every day to check in with her. Most days Summer was grateful for it, some days she resented it. Renae said those were the days that the call mattered most.

'Just feeling a bit low today.' Summer knew not to tell

her about Francine and her crazy idea. Renae would say that was just the kind of talk Summer didn't need.

'Maybe you need to get out more. Go to more meetings, meet more people.'

'I'm too tired for that.'

They'd been through all this before. Renae felt that recovery from a drug addiction affected a person's motivation. Without the drug she would find even day-to-day tasks exhausting and tedious.

'I've been thinking about my mum,' Summer said.

'That's good. What about her?'

'Just, you know, her addictive behaviour. How it's affected me. I think I miss the drama of being an addict.'

'Ha, yeah,' Renae's voice sounded wistful. 'But you're just gonna have to find new things to engage yourself, that's all, it's a big lifestyle shift.'

'I feel like I've spent my whole life just trying to patch up the holes of my childhood, fill them, you know, with drugs, sex, whatever stupid shit I could think of.' She watched on the television as they revealed the transformed rooms to the homeowner's shock and elation. That was always her favourite part of the show. 'I mean, is that what everyone's doing? In some way or another?'

'Well, not everyone, I guess, but not everyone had an alcoholic mother and a father they never met. You got a lot of holes, my dear.'

'It's just… I don't know,' Summer shifted herself to sit upright on the couch, she forced her eyes away from the TV screen.

'Don't know what?' Renae asked.

'I just don't see how long it can all go on like this.'

After she hung up Summer went to the bathroom mirror. She curled up her lips and squinted her eyes into hard little slits as she surveyed her teeth. Many of them had fallen out, the rest jutted out of her gums like rotting brown tombstones, reaching up in repulsive desperation. It really was something out of a horror movie, she thought, right there in her very own mouth.

***

Seabourne was one of those well-ordered, over-manicured suburbs that always made Summer feel uneasy. But today was different; she felt as if she owned everything around her and she surveyed it like a newly acquired possession. It was impressive, but at the same time she thought there was something fruitless and ornamental about all its beauty.

It was eleven a.m. and not another human being was in sight; only an SUV in the distance, shiny and sleek, sped down the wide empty road beside her car. She looked at her hands on the steering wheel, large bulbous knuckles, stumpy fingertips that were worn and calloused. Her gaze moved from her hands up to her wrists and her scarred and pockmarked arms. Their state was the product of all her decision-making, good and bad, and so were her teeth. No one else's fault but hers.

She looked across the road to the house; a white art-deco monstrosity, framed by severe square hedges and an equally severe section of front lawn. Inside, she knew, was a pomeranian and the biggest crystal chandeliers she'd ever seen.

The smell of old money came to her nose as she stepped through the lounge-room window. Summer knew it well: lavender mixed with something woody. The pomeranian attempted to bark but it came out in husky coughs. It was old and blind and, when she reached down to pat it, was already wagging its tail. It remembered her.

She walked through the master bedroom to the walk-in robe. At first she couldn't see the silver shoebox, but as she stepped further in she saw a corner of it poking out from under the ornate dressing table. She picked it up and opened it. It was full of rolled-up wads of fifty and one-hundred dollar notes. Being vigilant not to look at her reflection in the dressing table mirror, she opened up the top drawer of the dresser and gathered up all the watches. She slammed the drawer and saw the little dog in the bedroom cock its head. It sniffed the air, trying to assess what was going on with one of its last remaining senses.

She took three handbags from the back of the wardrobe door and stuffed the shoebox and watches inside one. She stopped for a moment as she crossed the bedroom again. Breathing it all in, the draping opulence of the curtains, the luxury of the high, billowing, freshly made bed, the soft-edged furniture everywhere. There was nothing utilitarian or practical about the place, nothing to suggest any exertion. Nothing but obscene cleanliness and luxury. She gave the dog a scratch then left through the front door.

Getting rid of stolen goods was the difficult part. Summer knew that was where Francine would have come unstuck. Francine would have tried to take it to hock shops or, even more ridiculous, sell the stuff on eBay. Summer drove straight to an industrial area on the opposite side of the city. She knew the wife of a bikie who dealt in luxury designer labels.

***

That afternoon, the sun was setting over the rooftops of the housing developments as Summer pulled into Francine's driveway. The suburb was quiet after all the excavators and front-end loaders working a few streets away stopped for the day. Every day they scuttled and chipped away like crabs at a sandy and ever-expanding shoreline of housing.

Francine and the kids shuffled out into the front yard as Summer got out of her car.

'It's a beautiful night out,' Francine said.

The two of them looked over to the orange sky. The baby and the youngest boy padded naked towards her. Summer picked up the youngest, tucking the plastic shopping bag full of money under her arm.

'I'm just making dinner,' Francine said, 'you wanna stay?'

'Nah, just stopping for a minute.' She put the baby down, saying she needed to use the toilet.

Summer went through the house to Francine's bedroom. The bed was littered with soft toys and the top sheet was crumpled at the end of the bed. Summer put the toys in a basket in the corner. Then she pulled up the sheet and tucked it into the mattress. She found the doona on the far side of the bed, aired it then let it fall, square and plump, on top of the sheet. She put the plastic shopping bag under the pillow, on the side with all the books and papers and a half-drunk glass of water. Then she plumped up all the pillows. She stepped back and looked at the bed for any imperfections. There were none.

As Summer drove away from Francine's house she looked at herself in the rear-view mirror. Pulling her lips back she gave herself a wide grin. It was disgusting, the sight of her teeth, but also strangely intoxicating.

Drowning

Jessica sat in the front right-hand pew like she did every Sunday morning. In front of her was Mrs Dobra at the church organ. She played a sombre 'spirit builder' for those still entering the church. Jessica watched the old woman's gnarled fingers pressing hard on the keys. The woman had her eyes closed and her UFO-shaped hat seemed to weigh down her tiny wrinkled head.

Paul, from behind the pulpit, announced the first hymn and there was a rustle as the congregation turned to the page and rose. Mrs Dobra opened her eyes to the music in front of her. Jessica stood up, her body feeling as stiff and wooden as the old jarrah pew beneath her. She had been running hard yesterday, longer and faster than she had ever before. When she ran she imagined herself running from a tidal wave that was just on her heels; if she stopped or slowed down, it would engulf her.

She looked up at Paul, who was belting out the first stanza of the hymn, articulating each phrase, moving his mouth with a force that showed he believed every word. Paul hated half-hearted singing, especially when it came to praising the Lord. Jessica mimed along, too tired for pushing out any sound. She smelt Mrs Dobra's musky Avon scent and looked longingly at her padded seat. Another hour of this, she thought. She couldn't remember the last time she'd had a proper night's sleep.

When everyone had sat down, Paul said, 'Let's turn to Mark chapter three, verse five.' Jessica held the Bible in front of her and let it fall to the book of Mark. She brushed at the thin, gold-edged pages to chapter three. She knew the verse, she knew the entire premise and conclusion of the sermon before Paul had even begun. Her index finger moved down the page to verse five, which read: 'He looked around at them in anger, being grieved by the hardness of their hearts.'

The more on fire he gets the more it feels like I'm drowning, Jessica thought, and a vision from her childhood came to mind. A scrub fire had got out of control and was threatening the house she and her mother lived in. The hose hadn't reached and the two of them, still in their pyjamas, ran with buckets back and forth from the rainwater tank to put it out. She hadn't even known her own strength, that she could carry two full buckets of water. She couldn't have been older than twelve. The moment she'd seen the fire brigade come up the street, her legs had buckled under her and she'd dropped down on the driveway in exhaustion, water from one of the full buckets pouring out onto her.

She looked up towards the pulpit now and surveyed Paul's ruddy face, the stubble that had itched her neck so rigorously last night. His chunky features and big shoulders were better suited to physical labour than the cerebral labours of the Bible. She watched the hairs on the side of his neck, they were strong and flat, like something fierce was gathering beneath the skin, like something angry was sprouting. She looked up at the small half-curved window to the patch of blue outside, wondering what other people were doing on a Sunday morning. She wished she could be out running now. It felt like a very carnal thing to long for, like something primal within her she couldn't help, but it was a longing of the flesh all the same.

That evening Jessica went out to the kitchen to put the kettle on. The Bible study was almost over and they were closing in prayer. She got out ten cups and lined them up on the kitchen bench. She looked at the clock. Five past ten. That's all she seemed to do lately, look at the clock, look at the clock. What was wrong with her, that she found it all so ... so boring? Every night there was something – prayer meetings, Bible studies, dinners. All she seemed to do was wait for it to end.

Paul came into the kitchen talking with George and Rosie. 'Hey Jess, what d'ya reckon we go down and help these guys at the outreach centre in a fortnight? Three days, it'll be fun.'

Jessica had her back towards them, facing the boiling kettle, so no one could see the ugly grimace that shot across her face. She had wanted to get her assignments for her design course done on the weekends. Somehow that now seemed selfish and frivolous compared to helping the poor and godless at the outreach centre.

'I suppose,' she said, pouring the boiling water into cups.

'You and Rosie can run the young women's group on Thursday night,' Paul said.

'Oh great, it'll be so nice to have you there, Jess,' Rosie's voice was always high-pitched and ridiculous.

Jessica turned and smiled at Rosie. She and George were the same age as Jess and Paul, and that seemed to mean they had to do everything together. Jessica got tired of their endless goodwill and praising God. They were like perfectly behaved children trying desperately to impress their parents or gain some prize, but they were pushing thirty now and Jessica could see right through it. She also secretly harboured a feeling that Rosie had brain-damage;

once at dinner Rosie told them a story about how she almost drowned in a swimming pool. 'The doctors all said I'd have permanent brain-damage,' she'd boasted, 'but, praise God, by his grace, I'm just a bit forgetful!'

Paul closed the door after the last of them had left. It was ten forty-five. Jessica groaned and slumped back towards the kitchen. 'God, they stay so long.'

'Why are you like that?' Paul's voice was sharp and quick. 'Like what?'

'So unwilling to give of yourself, so ... self-absorbed.'

'We devote every waking hour to others, Paul. You can't call me self-absorbed.'

'But you do it so unwillingly; you may as well not do it at all.'

'I'm not unwilling, Paul, I'm just ... tired.'

'Well, God's put us here to be a rock for these people. That's a real privilege. Serve the Lord with gladness, re-member Pastor Chris's message? That was a good message.'

'I know. I'm just not feeling the gladness right this minute.' She smiled and touched his shoulder as he passed.

'Pray about it,' he said. She nodded.

In bed she lay with her eyes open. She hadn't prayed for two years, but she hadn't told Paul that.

Often she was asked to pray for others in group situations, a terrifying and humiliating proposition, which she always managed to handball to someone else at the last minute. Praying made her feel silly, like she was talking to air. She tried to tell herself it was just like some kind of positive affirmation exercise or that if she prayed long and hard enough she might feel something. But she'd always just get lost in her own head and end up thinking about something entirely different – the words to a song, the name of a kid she went to primary school with.

***

When she walked into church the following Sunday, straight away she could tell something was not right. The two men stood at the back of the congregation. The cut of their shirts was soft and cottony, the creases in the back of their suit jackets indicated a linen blend – not right, she hadn't seen men wearing linen for a long time. The way their suit jackets hung off their broad shoulders. When she got to the front pew she turned around to look at their faces. She recognised them immediately. They were the two with the white dog, they walked by the river every day where she ran, and they were most definitely, without a doubt, she had concluded in her mind – gay.

She chewed the side of her mouth, a flutter of excitement tingled under her tongue. Gays, in her church? she thought. She found herself brushing her hair away from her ears and standing up a little straighter. She looked down at her outfit – fitted pencil skirt with a white shirt. She had her red heels on in an act of rebellion; they went with her red lipstick and nails.

Paul was already laying out the bones of his sermon, but she wasn't listening. What stupid fantasies were going through her head? Did she want to seduce one of these men? A hot flush of embarrassment came up her neck. What was she doing? Was she attracted? She couldn't be.

After the service, she avoided all eye contact with the back of the room, she went straight for the kitchen to help the women set up morning tea. As she put out the teacups she hoped that they would leave without the traditional after-church mingle, but then she heard Mavis Cox at the door saying, 'You must at least try some of Mrs Dobra's lemon slice.' What was the old bitch doing? Couldn't she see they were two gay men? They couldn't believe in God, a God that hates them. Jessica saw the teaspoon shaking as she brought a scoop of coffee to her cup. Imposters, she thought, would they sniff her out? Did it take one to know one? She put her coffee cup under the urn at the end of the table. Mrs Dobra took the glad wrap off her lemon slice and placed it next to the biscuits Jessica had arranged earlier. Then she saw the dark-haired one's arm reach across the table to grab a cup, his light blue shirtsleeve perfectly framing his tanned, beautifully formed, gay hand. She felt the air change around her. The cup shook in her hand, she didn't even want a coffee. What she wanted was to escape through the door at the back of the kitchen.

'I've seen you,' she heard him say, 'you're the runner.' A well-practised, easy smile came to his face, and Jessica felt a sharp twinge in the back of her throat. 'We own the white dog,' he said, reassuringly.

'Oh, oh yes.' Her eyes flitted across his face, but she didn't make eye contact. She couldn't.

Why? she thought. Why come here? This was her place to be an outsider; she didn't need more outsiders coming in, noticing her outsiderness. She looked up at his neck. At the park she'd noticed that neck; he was thin, but in a fine, tapered way – not too thin. She looked up at his eyes, which she knew were kind; they'd looked at each other before. What threw her was the way he fixed his eyes on her. It had thrown her at the river, too. When he looked at her, he *really* looked. It was like he was unpacking every one of her secrets, laying them out on the table in front of them, considering each individually.

'This is Jessica, our wonderful preacher's wife.' Loudmouth Mrs Dobra sensed the awkwardness in that bemused way old women do.

He blinked, a hard blink, and his face flinched like an

insect had flown into it. It was fleeting, but she caught it – was it surprise? A line of perspiration made its way down the back of her neck, under her heavy sheet of hair.

'Right, well it's very nice to meet you, Jessica.' He held out his hand and smiled knowingly; yes, it was – knowingly. Perhaps it was just that they'd never met formally. She didn't know, she took his hand, that big tanned hand, and felt her whole body being drawn into it, sucked in, not only to his hand but his eyes and his clean, distress-free voice. 'I'm Gary,' he said. She felt her face go into red blotches – she knew when that happened, it was all over.

***

On the following Sunday night they left the outreach centre at six fifteen p.m. Jessica felt too exhausted to move and the two-hour car trip ahead looked like a welcome rest. Paul still seemed full of beans, like the more he gave the more energy he got in return, like he'd been drinking energy drinks all day instead of talking about the Bible nonstop. Closing the door of the car, Paul started off down the highway. Something about her all-over-body exhaustion made her feel bolder and her problem seemed like it was a solitary candle in her hollowed-out mind.

'I can't do this anymore,' she said.

'Do what?' Paul sounded perky and chuffed with himself.

'All of this.' She waved her hand around manically in front of her. 'All this church stuff. I can't keep doing it.'

'Church stuff? This is our life, this is our reason for being on earth.'

'It's your reason, not mine. I don't know these people.' She sounded slightly crazy, even to herself.

'Three years we've been leaders in this church. What

do you mean, you don't *know* these people?'

'I don't know them, I don't *get* any of them, I don't get ... God.'

Paul's knuckles were extremes of pink and white on the steering wheel. He pulled over into a gravel parking bay.

'Jessica, I don't understand you.' He turned and looked at her and Jessica thought it was the first time he had done that in a long time. But he didn't look at her the way Gary had. Paul seemed to see her only through some kind of cheesecloth of confusion.

'No, you don't. You don't even know me. You've gone off down your God path, and left me behind here. Hello. Here I am!' she waved an insane, frenzied wave.

'Jessica, you're my wife.'

'Wife? What a stupid word. You've just got one coz everyone else has one and it makes you look the part.' Her voice came out harsh and grating. She thought it was her real voice, her voice without the soft polish and buffing she usually applied to it.

'That's, that is not true. I'm sorry if you think I've left you behind, but God is doing things in my life, our life.'

She yelled, 'God? I don't even *believe* in God!' The silence between them felt good and clean. She had said it, finally. She clenched her teeth in satisfaction and looked out the windscreen to the road ahead.

'I don't believe you, Jess.'

'Well, you better.' She squinted through the windscreen again. The thought crossed her mind of what she would do. The last thing Paul would want is a divorce. The thought of moving out exhausted her.

'I don't believe you'd say that after all God has done for us.'

'Well, it's the truth.' She felt the corners of her mouth

curl up in a smile against her will.

'You just need time, to, I don't know, get right with the Lord.'

***

Jessica closed the door behind her and started a slow jog towards the river. It was six a.m. and the sun was just peaking its way over the tops of the trees. She saw the river in front of her; the sight of that constant, reliable body of water always made her face and eyes relax. Although she still felt that burning drive, that impetus to run, something about this morning was different. She noticed the satisfying force of her sneakers on the grass. She felt every stretch and pull of her muscles. Her joints felt strong and agile. She was made to run, built to run.

Today, she didn't care if people believed in God. Good for them. Just as long as they weren't bothering her, and from now on, they wouldn't be. Somehow, her jaw felt loose and the muscles in her neck were supple, like they were no longer grinding tight and angry against her skin. She could notice the things around her – a row of purple flowers against a red leaf bush, two big pine trees reaching up to the wispy clouds above. This was all hers to enjoy, no one could stop her. She felt that sharp tingle on the surface of her skin, the feeling she always got when running, and she heard herself whisper, 'Perhaps that's God.'

Preparation

I pass the town hall clock, driving forty-two kilometres an hour. Petrol is 92.7 cents. Car has done 107,000 kilometres. It's thirty-seven degrees Celsius.

That's the kind of person I wish I was, preoccupied with the tedious and minute, the small and day-to-day. That kind of thing would keep me going, not angst-ridden over the big picture, obsessing over my position in the world. If I could just focus on the little things.

Behind me the town hall clock ticks on, and even with the air-conditioner on there is the shimmering terror of the heat outside.

Before me lies that haphazard last frontier of urban sprawl – Midland. Liquor stores and chemists prevail. This is what living hand-to-mouth looks like. No one planned or had any foresight of design when they built this place. It's like someone tried in a panicked way, in housing development after housing development, to cover up all that terrifying space that surrounds the city.

All the roads seem to begin and end here – the Great Eastern Highway, Great Northern Highway, Roe Highway. It doesn't exactly make it a serene place for living, but the fact that you can head in whatever direction you want and keep driving until there is nothing and no one may bring solace to some.

When people fly into Perth I can imagine them seeing the line of yellow sand and bulldozers and concrete pads that surround the outer suburbs like the shoreline of an island. All around this edge, children grow up with the smell of wet concrete and fresh paint, of newly levelled earth and the white hum of sprouting streetlights.

The honking of horns and the slowing of cars disturbs my reverie and on the side of the road I see a woman leaning against a white Commodore. She is dressed in a scanty white-leather cowgirl outfit and is smoking a cigarette in true Wild West style. The top of the outfit is really just a bra with tassels that reveals a flat brown abdomen and two mounds of heavily oiled cleavage. As I get closer I realise it's Nikki. I indicate and pull over a few metres in front of her, watching in the rear-view mirror as she grabs her handbag and marches towards my passenger door.

Nikki pulls her middle finger at several men in cars and trucks who beep and whistle as they drive by. A highly excited man in a fluoro shirt screeches out of a truck, 'Lost your pony, babe? I'll give you a ride!'

As she gets into my car I notice her arse is in full view. She is wearing cowboy chaps that have two round holes at the rear, from which her bum cheeks protrude in a very unwholesome way.

'For fuck's sake.' She throws her bag on the floor and slams the door. 'Why anyone can't put petrol in that piece of shit.' Sweat bubbles teeter apprehensively all over her perfectly applied make-up. 'I'm late for this show now, and it's so fuckin' hot!'

I indicate my way back into the sluggish catastrophe of bonnets.

'Can you just drive me to the footy club? It's gonna take forever to get petrol. Look at this traffic.' She holds out an upturned palm in disbelief at the jungle of trucks and utes around us, then she takes off her white cowboy hat in a sombre gesture, like she's at the funeral of some country and western singer. Her hair-sprayed blonde wig remains perfect and unmarred. Hours of preparation, I think, hours of preparation for life instead of actual real *life*. All that time she and I spent getting ready for our lives – how else could we have used that time? Studying carpentry? Making papier-mâché houses? Becoming neuroscientists? The possibilities were endless.

'Here I am,' she throws her hands up, 'back working for these bastards again. I got no money, no good orderly direction as they say in AA, and I'm in Midland.' She grunts in despair.

'Why don't you just quit?' This is a suggestion I have made often. She had quit once to start her own pole-dancing company, but it's hard to compete against the bikies' monopoly of the exotic dance industry.

'You'd think I coulda at least made it outta here by now, you know?'

'Well, Midland – it's not an easy place to … get out of.' It's true, I think as I look around. I glance back at Nikki, whose sweat beads have evaporated in the cool of the car's air-conditioning.

'It's just unbelievable how much I have stuffed my life up. I'm just fuckin' amazed by it.'

'No, you've done some good things.' It sounds feeble even to me.

'I'm nearly thirty. Nearly thirty! I'm still stripping. I'm still single, can't even find a half-decent guy.'

Nikki has what I've noticed many females in their twenties have – the idea that upon turning thirty their lives will suddenly end and they will completely disappear into the oblivion of old age.

'I mean, what's wrong with me?' She looks over at me with furrowed brows as if I am holding back some secret from her. I'm not sure, but I think being touched up by her father for all those years hasn't helped her in any rational decision-making process.

'You haven't had it easy,' I say.

'Well that's no excuse.'

'I know, but ...'

'I mean, you just have to look at how messed up my parents are. I mean yeah, what chance did I have? Huh?'

'You've done pretty well, all things considered.'

'Yeah well.' She stops. Tears are welling up in her eyes. She purses her lips together in an attempt to stop her chin from trembling. If she's not careful, tears will fall onto her perfectly made-up face. Outside, the glare and heat are all consuming, everything looks about to crack and sizzle, like a photograph put too close to a fire. As we come to the Roe Highway intersection you can see east to the hills with their precariously placed mansions looking down on us.

'I mean, why are we so fucked up?' She manages, somehow, to drag me down to the pits of despair with her. 'There are people out there with loving husbands and families. They've got money and drive around in, in ...' she waves her hands around her head in exasperation, 'in cars that have petrol in them!' A single tear makes its way down her face. 'How come we've missed the boat so well?'

I of course have no desire for husbands or happy, loving families, but Nikki often forgets this, believing it to be the aspiration of all females without exception.

'You should quit stripping. It's not good for your self-esteem,' I say. But I know Nikki is pretty much programmed to be a stripper, a hooker, a porn star, whatever. Most of the strippers I've met have been sexually abused.

'I mean, you don't even have a job, you don't have a boyfriend. I don't understand. Why did we miss out?'

'I don't know, Nik.'

'And now, you got all the bikies on your arse. You know, that's another thing.'

I'm not at all surprised at how fast news sweeps around Midland.

She sniffs up her crying and wipes away the one rebellious tear with a long acrylic fingernail. 'D'ya reckon you can give me something?' She grabs the rear-view mirror to assess the damage to her make-up. 'Those bastards have gone all tight-arse on me again, say I'm too much of a *good-time-girl*, fucking *good-time-girl*? I'm not even having a good time!' her voice cracks like she's gonna cry again.

'In my bag, side pocket.' I give it to her because I know I couldn't get up and take my clothes off in front of a football team without being high. I give it to her, but I tell myself this is the last time.

We have finally gotten through Midland's peak hour and up ahead of us is the hill. The lights turn green just as Nikki is snorting the crystals from her fingernail. After she finishes she lights up a cigarette and puts the window down.

'What you need is a man.' She puffs on the cigarette and looks out the passenger window towards the slow-moving traffic to the north.

'I don't need a man. There's men around; what do I need 'em for?'

Nikki rolls her eyes. 'Lyden? That fag. He can't help you, not with those pricks you've upset.'

I want to probe, I want to know what level of reaction my dissident drug-dealing activities are having with bikies, but we are already approaching the entrance of the football club.

'So has Benno said anything?' I ask.

'He fuckin' hates you, Stace. I don't understand what you did, or why, but ...' she shakes her head while taking a succession of long fast drags on the cigarette. 'You should find out who your dad is, maybe that's why your life is so fucked.'

'Yeah, because having a dad really helped *you*.'

She opens the passenger door while the car careens across the car park to the front door of the football club. 'I could be in serious trouble, you know, talking to you.' She slams the car door and I watch her walk toward the hall, teetering in her white stiletto cowboy boots. Her bum cheeks are out for all the world to see, the fake leather chaps glaring at my eyes in the sun.

I don't know what bugs me more: the fact she thinks I need a man to sort my problems out, or that she thinks I've 'fucked my life up'. Look where playing by the bikies' rules got her, I think, watching her saunter through the front door.

But as I turn the car around in the parking lot, a fear leaches into the groundwater of my brain. Maybe Nikki is right, maybe my life is comprehensively and irreversibly messed up for the simple misfortune of being female in a town ruled by men. As I drive back down the hill, a singular question turns over and over in my mind: Who the hell do I think I am?

Spiral

I saw him first. On the side of the road as we drove past. I saw him take hold of the bike handles, teeter, then fall and land on the sidewalk. I saw all the kids from the youth centre crowd around him as he scrambled like an insect on its back, hands and legs whipping in slow motion though the air.

At the time it was just another passing scene from the comfort of the passenger window. It wasn't until we were past the football oval and the public toilets, gliding down Morrison Road, that Tony whispered in disbelief, 'That was my dad.' He made a scrambling motion at the steering wheel that sent the car into a screeching, immediate U-turn. We had the trailer on the back because we were moving out of that dump, that dump that I now miss, where even going to the shops was an exercise fraught with tension. Where the police passed by a brawl or even an act of road rage as if it were nothing more uncommon than somebody pruning a rosebush.

Tony might not have noticed his dad if he hadn't sort of half-subconsciously been looking for him; his dad being in the midst of one of his downward spirals which involved him being found in new and humiliating displays of drunkenness and desperation – passing out in the doorway of his smallgoods shop, crying to the receptionist at the printing business a few doors down, abusing the bottle shop attendant who refused him alcohol. The whole reason he had taken to bike-riding was because, a month before, he'd been done for driving under the influence.

Each year the spirals would reach lower and lower depths; so low and so deep, it was like he was drilling down into the earth's surface looking for something.

It had been the mainstay of my arguments with Tony for the past few weeks.

'You've got to stop trying to *save* your parents,' I'd say, 'you've got to take care of yourself.'

'But what if something terrible happens?' Tony would reply. 'Imagine how I'd feel.'

We pulled up on the kerb in front of the youth centre. Tony's dad was standing now, swaying in the hot easterly breeze. His shirt was ripped and there was blood on his already mangled right hand, the hand he had cut in half in a work accident thirty years ago.

At first he didn't notice us pull up, he was too busy trying to offer a soggy, mashed-up bag of mandarins to the group of kids around him. His bike lay on the ground, the spokes bent from where he had landed on them.

'D'ya know 'im?' one of the taller boys said. 'We tried to help, but he's fallen off about ten times.'

Ignoring the boys, Tony said in his language, 'Why are you doing this?' He didn't yell but his words had this piercing, inappropriate sound that made all the surrounding boys look away; some looked to the ground, some inched backwards towards the youth centre.

He didn't answer Tony's question; his eyes went from us, to the boys on his left. That we were all there together seemed to confuse him, like we all knew each other, some conspiracy against him. He picked his bike up from the pavement and clutched onto the handlebars.

Cars roared past, V8s, hotted-up utes sans mufflers, trucks and red-dust-laden 4WDs. This was a place where the cackle of a loud modified engine gave people a feeling of warmth and comfort. The idea that car companies all over the world were busily trying to engineer motors to sound quieter seemed ridiculous.

When we got him to the car his confusion continued. He couldn't understand why we had the trailer on.

'Where are you going? Where are you going with this trailer on?' He looked up at us, and the look on his face was, in a way, childlike, but it was more like there was an actual child inside of his old man body, like a small child had somehow been surviving inside him all this time. We had told him before that we were moving, that for the first time in our lives we were getting away from the place where we grew up. We'd explained it all to him.

He finally let us have his bike, which we threw on the trailer. But still he kept trying to convince us he could ride home.

'You've already embarrassed yourself enough,' Tony spoke in English now. 'How much more do you want?'

I could feel Tony's shame as he tried to push him into the back seat of the car. His father tried to put up a fight, but, unlike his sober self, his drunk self seemed small and helpless and weak. The loud cars going past became irritating and vindictive like laughter.

'I make my own way home!' he yelled as Tony slammed the door on him.

Tony got in the driver's seat. 'It's six o'clock,' he said into the rear-view mirror. 'You close at four. What have you been doing?'

'I just talking with George.'

'Fuck George, I don't even wanna hear that dickhead's

name anymore.' Tony slammed his door. George was a local alcoholic, intent on guzzling as much booze as he could before he died of the asbestosis he'd been diagnosed with.

We took off down the road again. In the car the smell of alcohol and sweat was as pungent as one of those old public bars; the ones my mum used to drink in, the ones that all seem to have been gentrified now.

Tony's dad kept trying to open the car door while we were moving. Tony pulled over, bouncing over a kerb. This time I got out, walked around and put the child lock on the door. I looked down at the old man there in the back seat. I wanted him to feel something terrible. I wanted him to beg us for forgiveness. I wanted to tell him he'd be better off dead. I caught a glimpse of my face reflected in the glass, my eyes squinted into harsh slits, my mouth a pinched mean grimace. I'd become one of those people, I thought, those people whose anger oozes out of every pore of their skin, whose resentment covers every gesture, every stride they make through life.

As we drove I looked out at the squat, unkempt suburban houses and wondered how many other children were taking care of their drunken parents, how many other kids were looking for them, waiting for them to come home, just hanging on until they sobered up. My mother couldn't think straight with or without alcohol. She was really only a functioning adult for a few minutes a day – in-between opening her first bottle of wine and finishing her second glass of it. The rest of the time she was a ghost weighed down by the heavy chains of the past and the loneliness of not being a real, living person.

There was the obligatory yelling when we got to Tony's parents' house; his mum was furious. I couldn't understand much of it, as she doesn't speak English, but I learnt a long time ago the pointlessness of yelling at drunk people. I sat down for a few minutes on the couch while Tony tried to calm the situation. In the middle of it all Tony's dad came out to the lounge room, smiling, jolly almost – oblivious to the emotional shit-storm around him. He patted me on the head, ruffling up my hair playfully.

As we drove away from the house I said to Tony, 'It's like the world got too heavy for our parents. Only drinking makes them forget about the load for a while.'

That night, as I cooked dinner, we argued. I was angry that Tony wasn't as angry as I was. I had taken care of my drunken mother for most of my life and at twenty-eight I had only just started counting the costs of having someone entirely dependent on me. I was tired, overweight and depressed.

'I mean, I don't see your three brothers rushing to help. No, they've got lives of their own; they've got boundaries.'

Tony stood in the lounge room folding washing with the TV on. 'Well, I guess my dad is doing the best he can.'

'So fucking what? Doesn't mean I want to be involved in him doing the pathetic *best* he can! Why is it your responsibility?' The way I saw it, we had been constantly lifting his dad and my mum up from the side of a cliff, when we ourselves needed some lifting up.

'You don't know what my dad has been through. He's an idiot, I know, but I feel sorry for him.'

'Well, feeling sorry for people doesn't help them; it just *enables* them to continue being pathetic and useless and a burden.' I was kind of tired of listening to myself, tired of talking about other people, tired of trying to solve other people's problems. I turned the sausages and gave them a stab with the fork. Tony came into the kitchen and pulled some knives and forks out of the drawer.

'I mean, I see what you're doing. I did it, and now I feel like I gave all my energy away. I have none left.'

'That's not true. You don't just get one container load of energy that you can use up.' He sat at the table. 'Energy – it's a renewable resource.' He smiled.

***

A week later Tony's dad went missing. He'd stumbled home drunk one evening and he and his wife had got stuck into each other. For weeks, in recognition of his fondness for drink-driving, she had been hiding the car keys in the third kitchen drawer. But at six p.m. she'd heard the car start up in the driveway and realised he had found her hiding spot. By the time she got out of the front door he was speeding off down the street.

She called Tony. Tony drove to all three liquor stores in town, then he drove to the one outside of town. He looked all over for the silver Ford Falcon that his father drove, the one with all the dents and scratches from previous drunken trips. He looked in car parks out the back of pubs, he looked in the shopping centre car parks, he even looked in the car park at the train station. Two hours later he came home unsuccessful.

I didn't say anything. Tony sat on the lounge-room chair, and concentrated on his phone as if willing it to ring. I tried to make small talk to get his mind off it all. I wanted to say: Don't waste your life. I wanted to say: If he wants to kill himself, let him. I wanted to tell him of all the times I'd worried about my mother and wondered where she was, about all the times I'd resigned myself to being an orphan.

Instead I busied myself making a new soup recipe and when I turned around to comment on the copious amounts of sour cream the recipe called for, I saw he was crying.

Shiny tears glistened all over his face. It was shocking to see the way his heavy shoulders heaved up and down with each massive sob, the way his thick, oil-stained fingers reached up to violently wipe the tears away. He looked over at me and said, 'What am I gonna do about him?' I went over and sat next to him. 'I mean, why is he so screwed up?' He gasped for breath in between sobs. It looked painful. 'He did so much for us; it's all just a waste.' Tears streamed down his face and congregated at his chin, forming a constant drip.

After a long time I got up to check the potatoes on the stove. Tony had stopped crying, and was now slumped in front of the seven-thirty news. I re-examined the soup recipe and saw it asked for horseradish, which I didn't have. I stood at the bench and thought about giving up on the whole endeavour of a new recipe. There was a shepherd's pie in the freezer. I looked at my watch; I could still make it to the IGA before eight p.m.

As I came out of the IGA with my one jar of horseradish I heard the sound of a car horn. It didn't stop or start the way horns normally do, but gave a consistent ear-piercing blast. I could see that a crowd had formed at the entrance of the shopping centre car park where the sound was coming from and I went over to look under the dim streetlight. Over the shoulders of fellow onlookers, I saw the dented and bruised silver Ford Falcon. Somehow the car had been driven at great speed over a high embankment and ended up half inside the raised garden bed at the shopping centre entrance. Tony's dad was still at the wheel. He had passed out, with his head resting on the horn button in the centre of the steering wheel. Steam came out from under the crumpled bonnet. The car headlights were smashed but still shining. The engine revved because, although he had somehow got the gears into *park*, his foot was still planted firmly on the accelerator.

A few straggly young boys near me had a giggle and I guess it would have been funny if it wasn't so unfortunate – passed out in the centre of town with your head resting on the horn, heralding to the entire neighbourhood your complete lack of dignity. I stepped forward from the crowd and wrenched the car door open.

'Hey,' I shouted, 'wake up!' I tugged at his shoulder. For a minute I panicked, thinking he might actually be dead. Maybe he'd had a heart attack – he'd been told not to drink or smoke after the last one. But soon he mumbled something that I couldn't make out.

I got his head and yanked it off the steering wheel, just to shut the noise up. That's when I heard the police sirens. 'C'mon,' I shook him, 'you gotta get out of this car.' I undid the seatbelt and grabbed his hand from his lap, the hand that had been mangled by the factory accident when he was nineteen. The factory accident had put him out of work for two years. It had stopped him tinkering, fixing things, stopped him playing piano. It was the factory accident that had started, possibly, his first downward spiral.

His head was now resting on the back of his headrest and, realising there wasn't much hope of me pulling him out, I sat down in the passenger seat and closed the door.

He looked over at me and sighed. Then he said, 'Sorry. I'm sorry.' His voice had a quiver to it that embarrassed me. I couldn't look at him. 'I know, I'm not good.' His English was never that great so I couldn't tell if he meant *it's* not good or *I'm* not good. He turned his head to look at the mess that was the front end of his car. 'Just sometimes,' he said, 'I feel so, *so* bad.' I looked back at his face, and there was something unexpected in his expression, something like hurt and surprise mashed together. I looked down at his mangled hand again and imagined for a moment that the nineteen-year-old, with all his dreams and aspirations, was somewhere inside his body. I thought maybe he got a glimpse of it now and then and tried, with the help of the bottle, to push it back down. I imagined his hope stretching back like an elastic band – further and further – being pulled taut until it was let go and he was flung back into despair.

As the blue lights of the police car came up behind us, his head dropped down to his chest and he was asleep again.

Playing Dead

When Rick's ute turned around and shone its headlights down the road, Diane jumped into the scrubby verge behind her. She was quick and agile like a cat. If she was cat-like, she thought, what kind of animal was Rick? A dog? A wild boar? She often compared people to animals. A by-product of growing up on farms; the traits of animals often more keenly observed than those of humans.

She crawled on her belly looking for a place to hide but there was little foliage, only the slight dip of the drain. Minutes before she'd been in the sweaty cab of the ute with Rick screaming, driving 110 down the gravel road. His voice was still ringing in her ears. It seemed to have grown louder, sharper over the years, until all she could do was jump, bolt, run, throw her body in any direction to distance herself from it.

Her nose was tickled by the wild oats, a rock dug into her right cheek, a piece of dead wood gouged at her stomach, but she let go of all these physical sensations because that's what you do when you're playing dead. Often she imagined she was on a stage in front of a darkened audience talking into a microphone: 'When you play dead, you have to lie flat and taut without breathing, it's a practised art, a kind of meditation.' She often imagined herself giving training seminars on it, complete with PowerPoint slides and photographic examples – *How to Pretend You're Dead: A Practical Guide.*

She had seen a lot of tiger snakes along this road, but somehow, lying on her belly in the ditch, awaiting Rick's violent wrath, a tiger snake didn't seem like much of a threat. At that moment a tiger snake seemed so domestic and benevolent that if one came by she imagined herself reaching out to pet it.

She concentrated on the sound of the ute moving down gears, its tyres crunching the gravel underneath, its diesel engine thudding loudly under the bonnet. It slowed down just near her face, idling fitfully like it was about to conk out. She held her body stiff and flat. She knew she couldn't hold her breath much longer; her temples began to thump in time with the clatter of the engine.

***

A week later she looked out on the yellowed paddocks that reached to the horizon. A single wattle tree, stunted and disfigured, sat in the centre of her view. Sheep congregated around it, hanging their heads in wait for the passing heat of the day. She let the dirty dishwater go and dried her hands on the tea towel. Seventeen years she'd been looking out on the same scene. Soon, she thought, she'd be faced with different views altogether, maybe looking out onto a street or a park, or the pretty lights of a city. The thought triggered a deep, almost painful breath and her teeth ground tight against each other. She had long ago trained herself to shut down any feeling of hope; like blocking out light in a darkened room, she closed herself off to the tiniest shard of it.

She looked over at the shed. Calling from the truck one night, Rick had asked her to turn on the water timer in there. That was when she'd first seen it, the grow room. She had known he was up to something; ever since he'd connected a backup generator and stockpiled several varieties of fertiliser months before. Since then, the farm – seven hundred acres and a thousand head of sheep – had fallen by the wayside. She'd known from the day she moved out here, Rick couldn't run a farm, you had to like hard work to farm anything, and Rick was what her father would have called 'work shy'.

The night he'd called from the truck, and when she'd gone and opened the newly installed door at the back of Rick's shed, hot bright lights hit her face. Low-hanging fluorescent tubes were dangling from the roof and below them was a sea of shocking green – violent, exotic green – green like she had never seen before. In front of her had been over a hundred full-size marijuana plants. Hot tears had pooled at her eyelids – the work! the achievement! Part of her thought: for once, he had gotten off his arse. The plants were so dainty and unexpected she had wanted to pull them all to her body and bathe in their soft, fine beauty. Then she felt rage itch at the back of her throat – after all she'd been through, he'd keep this from her?

***

Diane lay awake on top of the sheets and thought about the plants. The image of them was burned into her brain and they were often the last thing she thought of at night. She had done some research and she couldn't believe that one plant alone could be worth up to three thousand dollars. Rick lay next to her; she had never been able to get used to his loud and erratic snoring, which would always jolt her into terrified awakeness. She had to see them again, the plants, make sure they were still there, that she hadn't dreamed it all up. She needed to count them too – was there really a hundred? Or was it more like fifty? Or maybe it was two hundred. Lately, more nights than not, she stayed up fantasising about all the things she would do with the money, when she was free of Rick: shopping, plastic surgery, frivolous things like getting her hair and nails done. She knew these things wouldn't make her happy, but she thought they might pave a path, or be stepping stones to happiness or maybe even at least a distraction until she figured out what happiness actually was.

She tiptoed breathlessly out of the bedroom and down the hallway. She often felt proud of her physical agility. At forty-four, it was one of the few advantages honed from living with a man who might, at any moment, throw you at the nearest sharp object. In the kitchen, the light of the full moon reflected off the benchtop. She went into the pantry and took a single silver key hanging from a shelf, then crept out the back door towards the shed. The dog followed, half-asleep, out of instinct, and she patted his soft head. The heavy tin door of the shed squealed as she pulled it open. As she entered and pawed against the wall looking for the light switch, her eye caught on a sliver of light coming from under the doorframe at the back of the shed.

Only once had he mentioned the plants outright; half-drunk, in the heat of an argument, he'd screamed, 'Tell anyone about my plants, I'll fuckin' crush you, crush you like a bug.'

'Plants?' she'd asked, feigning ignorance, 'what plants?'

A year ago Rick had got Foxtel installed and this had taken up most of his waking hours. He'd started drinking earlier in the day. He had grown slow and fat and more irritable than ever. Being around the house with Rick was like trekking through a thick foreign jungle trying to avoid landmines. Now, she realised, Rick wasn't just hanging around, he was waiting. Waiting for the plants.

The fluorescent tubes above gave a delayed flicker before lighting up and she shivered. The old out-of-commission farm truck was in front of her, a big green F250. Three years ago she had been allowed to drive it, now she wasn't allowed to leave without Rick, she wasn't allowed to make a phone call without his supervision.

She weaved her way between paint tins and buckets of fertiliser and a quad bike, all the time being careful not to brush against anything and soil her nightie. She got to the back of the shed where she had seen the strip of light. Rick had installed the door and a new wall of gyprock covered the original back wall of the shed to make the room. She put the key into the large silver padlock on the door.

Then she heard Rick bellowing from the house. 'Diane?' he called out. Her jaw clenched and she bit the side of her mouth. She turned and hopped over the paint tins, bounded over bags of fertiliser, alert and nimble as a gazelle sensing a predator.

Just as she closed the shed behind her, the lights in the kitchen turned on. 'I'm out here babe,' she tried to sound light and sweet, taking all the terror out of her voice and putting it somewhere deeper and lower in her body. She patted the dog hard.

'What the fuck are you doing out there?' His voice like a chainsaw starting up.

'Just looking at the stars.' She threw the keys up into the air, ridiculously, trying to rid herself of them, her hands shaking. They landed near the stairs.

'Don't bullshit me,' Rick yelled, appearing at the back door, 'you get back inside.' The dog waddled away, tail between his legs.

She held her breath.

'GET INSIDE.' His scream seemed to make the whole

house shudder. Diane bounded up the stairs and through the back door. She felt his hand take hold of her neck as she came in. His hands were thick and coarse and her thin, ageing skin pinched under his fingers. It was a familiar sensation, predictable. She no longer felt cat-like, gazelle-like, only disgustingly human.

'You little slut, you were nosin' around my plants, weren't you?'

'I wasn't, hon', I just went out for some fresh air.'

'Don't you lie to me.'

She tried to turn her head to look up at him but could only see the bottom of his blue boxers and his hairy, sinewy legs.

'No, I just couldn't sleep. Honestly babe.' With his hand at her neck he pushed her forward and towards the floor. She was ready for that, managing to bring herself up from hitting the tiles. He went towards the pantry.

'Honey, I didn't go in your shed.' She was acting on instinct but she was lost. Maybe she should start running again – just bolt, her body didn't hold up against the beatings like it used to and what did she have to prove? As he swung the pantry door she made a leap for the back door again.

'You lying little *cunt*.' On the last word he made a punch for her and got her in the side. She hit the doorframe hard with her shoulder.

'Where's the key?' He grabbed her by her hair. She knew it was better to get this over with. In the early days she'd play dumb, deny his accusations, try to fight. She'd regretted that behaviour, especially since the kids had seen it.

'Bottom of the stairs,' she whispered. He dragged her down the stairs by her hair. She didn't bother with screaming anymore, it took too much energy. Only panting whimpers came out against her will as she tried to breathe.

'What the fuck is your problem, what do you want with my plants?'

She went limp under his hands. That's what you had to do, she'd learnt now, become pliable, submit.

'After all I've done for you.'

'Honestly, Rick, I didn't go in there. I was, I was looking for a torch. I wanted to go for a walk.'

'I don't believe a fucking word you say. *You* cannot be trusted.' She felt a rain of saliva on her shoulder as he spat out the words. 'You sit up in this house doing fuck-all while I provide a roof over your ugly fuckin' head, then you go sneaking around into my private business.'

'I didn't see your plants, Rick.'

'You'll never leave here, do you understand that?'

There was something unimaginative and tedious about the exchange. When she was younger, she thought with disgust, it had almost been exciting, never in a good way of course, but in a challenging sort of way, like if she could withstand his beatings and his violence she would be vindicated and worthy. But she couldn't imagine who she was trying to impress. Who would vindicate her? Rick? Even the kids had given up on her, and her sister and mother hadn't spoken to her in years. And what was she trying to prove? That she wasn't afraid of death? Or was it how stoic and tough she was? Her father had always seen that as a virtue; 'What doesn't kill you makes you stronger,' he used to say. It was a pretty crap saying, she thought now, definitely not one to live your life by.

'Are you listening to me?' he rattled her head around, 'I'll put you in the ground, you useless bitch. You're no good to anyone, even the kids don't wanna see ya no more.' She felt her hair coming out by the roots.

***

She woke up with bright lights in her eyes, the smell of bleach and the crisp hard cotton of the pillowcase on her face; she knew she was in hospital. Her first thought went to the plants. What time was it? Was it morning? Had he harvested them already while she was out of the picture?

'How long have I been here?' she asked a nurse coming into the room.

'Two days.' The nurse was stocky and had an efficient, brusque air about her. She stood at the side of the bed holding a file. 'You've got some serious injuries.' The nurse scanned her face. 'Who did this to you?'

'I fell.' She glanced at the nurse, sure one of them would laugh, but neither she nor the nurse cracked a smile. It wasn't much of a joke really, she thought, too clichéd.

'I need to leave here.' She tugged at the sheet folded tightly across her chest.

'You need to sit tight, my dear.' The nurse, fussing with the files and papers, looked at her. 'You know there is an excellent DV support service here in Merredin, they can provide you with accommodation.'

'I know. I'm leaving him. I have a plan.'

As the nurse left the room she caught the condescending curve that was still etched into the woman's mouth.

'Hey,' she shouted after her, 'you couldn't give me something to help me sleep?'

'I'll be back with something.' The nurse nodded and closed the door.

From her bed she looked out the window to the dried-out geraniums and the dusty white gums surrounding the car park. When she was a kid she had been the top of everything in her class, so quick and bright – she remembered happily all the praise, and the jealousy too. Maybe that had been her problem, why she didn't want to admit the truth now, why she'd been stuck out here so long. She was just too proud.

She did the sums in her head again, it had become a ritual, a little therapy exercise to calm her anxiety. Even if only thirty plants survived, she thought, and even if she sold them extra cheap, say a thousand dollars each, that was still thirty thousand dollars – thirty thousand dollars! She could get a deposit on a house, a car, get the kids back.

The next day she was discharged. Rick had somehow got wind of it; he was waiting for her in his ute out the front of the Merredin Hospital. He smiled and performed a self-conscious little wave that she recognised as the wave of the 'other Rick', the Rick who was gentle and charming. She sometimes imagined 'other Rick' dragged around, bound-up and restrained behind the seething, angry, irritable Rick who was always at the fore.

He was kind, bumbling, and when they got home he made her some cheese and tomato sandwiches and a cup of tea. 'They had a program on sloths on the tele,' he said. She loved sloths. 'Beautiful little creatures,' he shook his head. She wanted to cry, she wasn't sure if it was the vision of a sloth that had come to her mind, so slow and endearing, or whether it was how nice he was being to her. She took the dog's head in her lap and gave him a long pet.

She decided to take the dog for a walk. Across the paddock she veered off past the old shearing sheds. The sun was setting but still managed to throw its last sharp rays of yellow light into her face, and she squinted at the ground. The dry grass snapped and crackled under her thongs and filled them with grass seeds. Behind the shed she stopped and took out the extra sleeping pills the doctor had given her. She had three others that she had saved from the hospital. She put the capsules in the little plastic tube with the others. She knew she didn't have long if she was to get in and harvest the plants before Rick.

Two days later she was opening a can of Emu Bitter and dropping the insides of the capsules into it. In an hour he was sprawled in his recliner chair in front of the TV fast asleep. It was that easy.

She pulled out the bag she'd packed from the bottom of the wardrobe and ran out to the shed. She wound her way at full speed through to the back door. She had the key, pinched and trembling, between her thumb and forefinger.

She took from her bag the big meat knife she'd sharpened from the kitchen and began slicing the plants low down on the stem. She threw them at the door, one after the other. They piled up quickly; in eight loads she took all 134 plants out to the ute, knocking herself on all the accumulated crap in the shed, upturning tins of paint and bags of fertiliser. The plants bulged up under the tarp she fastened over them, and she had to strap them down with a rope. She called to the dog, which jumped on to the passenger seat. She slid into the driver's seat and turned the key.

She hadn't driven in a long time and as she went out the front gate she remembered how much she loved the feeling of the steering wheel in her hand, the night air blowing in her face through the window. She rested her elbow on the windowsill and felt a painful bubble come up her throat. At first she didn't realise what it was. Then she knew, it was a laugh.

She needed to put as much distance as she could between her and that farm. She needed lights, she needed noise, she needed people. Never again would she be trapped in a prison of such endless, terrifying space.

The ute bounced down the gravel road and she thought of Rick waking up in his armchair, tied up with his own rope, every inch of him desperate to rush out to his plants. She screwed up her face at the thought. She looked down at the dog, its black eyes reflecting the headlights, its big brown face almost exploding with joy.

The Tower

In front of the mirror, Beth pouted. She couldn't take her eyes off her glossy, flawless lips. She pulled back her hair from the side of her face and jutted her chin out. The Ruby Red lipstick always mesmerised her.

Beth spent a lot of time looking in the mirror. Sometimes she thought she was like the girls in the magazines and that meant she was beautiful. Other times Beth thought she looked grotesque and should try not to leave the house too often. Most of her days were balanced between the two. Beth didn't know, couldn't decide. It was a fine line and it all depended on how many times and in what light she gazed at her reflection.

All through the house there were pictures of her mother in her youth – modelling shots in black and white, framed magazine covers, elaborate poses against abstract 1970s colours. She found it hard to see her real, present-day mother in the photos. As she'd aged, her mother's identity seemed to fade, like the writing on a t-shirt that had been put through the wash too many times.

These days her mother took a lot of sleeping pills and was afraid of answering the phone. They lived in a small, falling-apart transportable on the outskirts of town. They'd moved out there to 'get away from it all', as her mother put it. Beth knew the town was full of people doing just that.

Beth had been home from school for over an hour. It was normal for her mum to sleep until teatime and she didn't like to be disturbed. She pulled back the bathroom curtain and through the cobwebs, across the paddocks, Beth could see the tower. It was made of two giant tank stands welded together, with three platforms and several ladders up the sides. Above the steel frame, far above the roofs of the tiny, piddly little town, bolted high on a steel pole, small and spindly so you had to really squint to see it, was an office chair, the type that swivels.

Beth remembered the day she had looked out the window and seen it for the first time. She thought of the tower as some kind of symbol; the man had built it as a stand against everything flat and boring around it, everything the town stood for. She smiled, thinking about the man, and as she did she felt as if she was lowering her body into a warm bath, she thought it was love or excitement but when the feeling passed her jaw clenched and she felt disgusted with herself.

She walked over to Jane's house. They sat on the bed under a picture of Axl Rose in amongst Jane's soft toy collection. Jane's pet lamb was splayed out on the floor next to them.

'Don't you ever want to just sit up there and look down on everybody?' Beth said.

'What?' Jane was reading the latest *Smash Hits* magazine while Beth was staring out the window.

'Up in the tower.'

'Not particularly,' Jane rolled her eyes.

'He'd probably let me if I asked.'

'That old pervert?' Jane pouted, 'he'd let you alright.'

'What do you mean, pervert?'

'What do you think he uses that tower for, stupid? He sits

up there perving through bathroom windows, watching us all hop out of the shower.' Jane flicked through the magazine with impatient hostility. 'Oh, they say he uses that tower to keep an eye on the refinery, make sure it's not overpolluting.'

'Doesn't he?'

'As if he cares about the refinery.'

'He is, kind of, different,' Beth said. She had seen the man at the petrol station sometimes. He was always alone, a quiet, short man with wild hair. He drove an old Holden ute which had a 'Stop Nuclear Testing' sticker on the back window.

'He is, kind of, *weird* you mean,' Jane replied. 'My dad says he's some kind of a survivalist; he's got all these conspiracy theories.' Jane sighed and placed the open *Smash Hits* magazine on the bed next to her. A picture of Johnny Depp stared up at them; he had an angry pout and a white bandana wrapped around his head. 'Oh, and he's a communist too.' Jane sounded authoritative, like she even knew what a communist was.

As the sun set, Beth walked home to make tea for her and her mother. She cooked sausages and boiled some cabbage and potatoes.

'How's school?' her mum asked, slouched at the crowded dining table, poking at her food.

'Good,' Beth answered, but she could see her mother wasn't listening by the way she stared, transfixed, at the beige linoleum tiles.

All around them were remnants of her mother's history, her short-lived modelling career. She got rid of nothing; it was all piled up high and covered with dust and cobwebs. Half of the dining table was submerged in unopened mail, papers and photo albums that her mum had been 'sorting' for years. The hallway was jammed with boxes of clothes gifted by the various designers her mother had modelled for. A mouse scurried out from one of them as they sat at the dinner table.

After washing up, Beth went over to the encyclopedia set on the lounge room shelves. She took out the M–O book and looked up *Nuclear Energy*, then she took the C–D book and looked up *Communism*.

The next day after school Beth walked to the perimeter of the man's property. She stopped at a section of the fence where the wire sagged low. Looking up from that angle the tower appeared terrifying and ridiculously high.

She wanted to go to the top, but also she just wanted to talk to him. Now that she knew what nuclear energy and communism were.

She stepped through the fence, her dirty farm sneakers sinking in the black sand. Up ahead she could see the massive green of the vegetable gardens. Giant dinosaur-like sprinklers stood immobile amongst the lines of vegetables. People said he had an underground tunnel with a bunker, people said he powered everything by the sun, people said he kept a lot of weapons. All Beth could see were solar panels on the roof of the A-frame shed, a lot of machinery and pumps – it looked just like a normal farm. The only thing different, she noticed, was that compared to the several shades of beige that coloured the town, this property was lush and green. It was like a little square of a foreign country had been taken up and transplanted here amongst the barren farms.

She gripped the ladder at the base of the tower and looked up. The chair at the top seemed to rock back and forward in the afternoon breeze. Then she heard whistling. Looking over the rosemary bushes she could see the man walking through the vegetable gardens with a rifle slung over his shoulder.

She crouched down in the bushes watching him pass. She thought about what Jane said, about him being a pervert. She remembered what her mum once told her, about how all men were only after one thing.

His halo of hair was what people in town knew him by. It formed a wiry bird's nest around his head, red and blond, with flecks of grey. It looked like he had gotten out of bed ten, maybe twelve years ago, and had never bothered to brush it since. He was short but thickset, like an old tree whose roots went deep into the ground. Beth thought of her mother then; tall and thin, she often reminded Beth of a sapling swaying all over the place, unsure of its survival in such inhospitable conditions, with such shallow roots.

She watched as he got closer to her, then he stopped and looked through the foliage. Glancing down, Beth realised she was wearing red shorts and a pink tank top, making it impossible to blend into the surroundings. She stood up. His face was fierce and ruddy.

'What are you doing?' he said, articulating each word.

'Just looking at the tower.' Her eyes fell on his tattered workboots. She wasn't used to men. No matter how much she imagined herself relaxed and in control, even interacting with her friends' fathers was a terrifying situation.

He snorted. 'You can *look* from your house,' his head shot up to the top of the tower behind her. 'You can *see* it from there.'

She kept her eyes on his workboots. Her heart seemed to be beating somewhere just at the base of her tongue, like she could vomit it out and it would be lying there on the ground between them, still pumping frantically.

'You were going up it.' It wasn't really a question but she nodded.

'Well, you just need to ask.' He was the same height as her, she could notice that much. And despite his sun-worn, beaten-looking face, there was still an alertness, something open that hadn't been shut.

He adjusted the rifle on his shoulder and nodded towards the tower. 'You wanna go to the top?'

Beth wasn't so sure she wanted to climb up now, but when he walked past her he seemed intent.

'You wanna see what the birds see, huh?' he let out a deep resigned breath as if he knew that's really what everyone – with no exception – wanted.

He leant his rifle against the steel railing of the tower stand. 'Well, up you go then.' He beckoned her towards the ladder.

Beth took in the rifle, the filthy shirt and face. This hairy, crazy-looking man in front of her telling her to come forward.

Jane was always angry that Beth never found any of the rock stars and movie stars in *Smash Hits* that exciting. 'What is wrong with you?' Jane would say, as if Beth was some kind of perverted lesbian because she didn't want to drool over another picture of Corey Haim. The fact that Beth found this man intriguing would have disgusted Jane.

The sun was setting; normally at this time of evening she would be making dinner. The man gestured again towards the ladder, this time with a chivalrous flourish, like she was a lady about to enter a grand ballroom. Something about his gesture and appearance seemed clown-like and endearing. She put her foot on the first rung of the ladder.

Within eight steps she was standing on the first landing. Looking behind she could see the small bald spot at the centre of his head as he came up the ladder. She imagined baby birds nested there, happily sheltered.

She breathed in the view all around her; the ground was getting dark with long shadows but the tops of the trees were still bright with different shades of green.

They climbed up to the second landing. It was a smaller space and that meant they had to stand with their arms touching. She could smell wet soil and sweat and the same feeling came over her, the one she'd had looking out the bathroom window.

Looking out from this higher vantage point, she felt her stomach sway. The sheep and fences looked too small. There was nothing – no barrier or even handrail – between her and those far-off fence posts. She crouched down and pressed her runaway stomach against her knees.

'I think this is far enough,' her voice came out in a high-pitched waver. 'I wanted to go to the top, but I don't think I can.'.

'Whatever you think.' He was now crouched down next to her, his eyebrows jutting across his face in a straight line. His concern made her feel even more panicked. She turned around on her hands and knees, her eyes fixed on her fingernails, thinking she might vomit. He took her arm as her left foot searched for the first rung of the ladder.

When they got back down to the ground he said, 'Next time you want to climb the tower, you come and ask, I don't want anyone hurting themselves.'

She rushed home and lay on her bed. She ran through the whole interaction in her mind, over and over. Everything he'd said, everything she'd said. She laughed and smiled then curled up on her side. She thought about his hands, thick and stained from manual labour. She imagined them rubbing her hair back from her face softly. Then she imagined them running up and down her arm. She imagined him telling her she was very beautiful and a feeling of supreme comfort and joy came over her. Then she heard her mother's footsteps on the floorboards. It was dark and she'd forgotten all about dinner.

The next day after school she went to the same sagging part of the fence and stepped over. He was in the vegetable garden harvesting broad beans.

'Hello again,' he said and smiled from where he was crouched next to one of the raised garden beds.

She smiled back. Without saying anything she picked up a plastic container nearby and began plucking fat broad beans from the next row.

When their containers were full she followed him into the A-frame building. Inside stood his ute and a long, ancient caravan. Machinery and tools and horse gear were stored on the far wall. It smelt of livestock and hay.

He took her to a long row of freezers against the shed wall and opened one of them. It was full to the brim with bagged-up produce. Above the freezers were lists taped to the wall; items had been ticked off: beans, corn, kale, spinach.

'What's all this for?' she asked.

'It's preparation.'

'Preparation for what?'

'In case something happens.'

'What might happen?'

'Oh, anything really, at this point in time.'

'Anything?'

'Sure, the world – well, this planet anyway – it's on its way out.'

'And you want to survive it?'

'I'll have to wait and see. I just know I don't want to starve to death when the shops don't open.' He smiled, slamming the freezer door down.

She wanted to ask more, but she had caught him looking at her a few times and she felt ashamed by the intense intimacy of the last hour, and her forwardness. She let her hair fall over her face and glanced down at her skinny, tanned legs. As soon as she could she scurried out of the shed into the orange-coloured dusk.

On her way home she imagined all the 'anythings' that could happen. She'd read about nuclear blasts and radiation poisoning in the encyclopedia. If he was prepared, she wanted to be prepared too.

When Beth got home she took out the S–U volume of the encyclopedia on the lounge-room shelf. She went to her room and read everything that was written under the heading *Sexual Intercourse*.

A few days later she saw him at the supermarket. She was with her mum on their weekly shopping trip. He nodded to her and the two of them exchanged secret little smiles. Beth's mother, too entranced by her own suffering, didn't notice the man or their interlude. But later, she said to Beth, 'You're always in a dream, what's the matter? Are you in love or something?' Beth didn't respond. She thought it was a reference to the supermarket exchange between her and the man, but then remembered that her mother always said that.

Beth started going to his house every day after school. One hot afternoon he split the biggest watermelon in the garden and they sat and ate and Beth told him about all the baby animals she had raised and where they had ended up – a sheep, a goat, kittens. He moved the hose every so often to water the vegetables.

It was so nice having someone listen to her and she was enjoying the sweet, crisp watermelon so much that between mouthfuls she spat out, 'I don't want to go home.'

He nodded. 'I noticed you keep coming over.'

'I like it here.'

'Why?'

'It's just nicer to have someone to talk to I guess.' She felt her face redden.

'Don't you talk to your mother?'

'Not really, she sleeps all day, pretty much.'

'Well, you're welcome here anytime.'

Beth felt a bubble of happiness rise up to her throat, so that swallowing the watermelon felt almost impossible. It sat in her throat for a long time.

'Let me show you something,' he said getting up. She followed him through the shed to a small open trapdoor in the floor. He grabbed a torch from on top of the fridge nearby, then lowered himself into the opening. Beth waited at the top. She knew Jane and her mum would tell her not to go down the ladder, but she also knew that nothing in the world would stop her.

Except for the torchlight, the space at the bottom was dark and Beth felt a tremor come up from her ankles to her knees like the ground underneath her was moving. The man turned on a gas lamp which revealed a small room full of books and boxes of food. A fold-out bed was against the wall.

'Take a seat,' he said. 'I'll make you some tea or something.' He put a kettle on a small camping stove and switched it on. Beth sat on the bed. She looked around at the bar fridge, the four-litre bottles of water that were stacked to the ceiling, the rice piled up in hessian bags.

'So this is my little hidey-hole,' he smiled and stood in

the small space in front of her, waiting for the kettle to boil. She examined his hands as they went into his pockets; his expression, which seemed a bit shy. She noticed the way his faded, loose jeans hung from his thick waist.

'You are welcome to come down here whenever you like.'

'It's pretty cosy down here,' Beth looked up at him. 'Definitely feels safe.'

'It *is* safe, it's twelve-inch concrete with steel and aluminium lining.'

But that wasn't what Beth had meant.

For weeks now, Beth had kept the S–U book of the encyclopedia under her bed. She had reread the entry on *Sexual Intercourse* over and over again and studied the two diagrams that showed men and women in the sex act. She knew she had to begin by touching him, that was the first step, and that seemed easy because it felt like even the hairs on her arm were reaching out towards him. She had read the subheading on *Sexual Arousal*. She didn't have a plan beside groping and gently pushing. All she knew was that she wanted him to like her, she wanted him to see she was someone special.

He brought the tea over and put it down on a crate. When he sat down next to her on the bed she could feel the heat coming off his body. A sweeping thrill passed through her body, like an avalanche of sand falling off a cliff face.

She put her hand on his leg and he jolted like her hand was something burning hot she'd put against him. Then, regaining his composure, he put his hand on her hand and shuffled closer to her. He ran his fingers up her arm to her shoulder. She leant in close towards him, touched the wiry, tangled hair around his face. It felt like steel wool.

His body felt rock-hard against hers, like there was no way anything could live inside it. She felt his weight pushing against her. Then he reached his hand to the back of her neck under her hair. The kerosene lamp in the corner of the room was dim. It was finally happening, she thought. Something big felt like it was beginning, like the whole of her life was really starting.

He kissed her and it was such a strange sensation that she wanted to laugh. She felt she was getting lost in it, in his mouth, like he was drawing her tongue out of her, unravelling it from its base, way down in her crotch. She smelt him – it was earth and hay and something sweet from a plant that she didn't know the name of. She felt his stubble on her skin and she decided that she didn't want to go home, ever.

Then he pulled back, looking at her with that same angry intensity as the day he saw her crouching behind the rosemary bushes. 'How old are you?' he asked.

'Fifteen,' she said.

He exhaled loudly.

He put his hand on her shoulder to push her back and she felt his body cool and deflate under her hands.

'I guess I should have asked. I guess I didn't want to.' He put both his hands in his lap and looked towards the light coming from the lamp. 'We can't do this,' he said.

'Why not?'

'Because you're not old enough.'

'I am.' She pulled him back towards her, but his body was limp and infuriatingly complacent.

'You're not old enough to make those decisions.'

Her cheeks burned like she'd been slapped.

'I want it. I want to do it.' Her voice came out too loud for the tiny room. She tried to pull his shoulders to face hers. This time he turned to her, but his expression was steely, hard, emotionless.

'I'm sorry,' he said, 'but this is just not right.' He pursed his lips and turned his head back to the lamp. 'I'm happy for you to be here, I know your home life isn't great and I really do enjoy your company, but maybe this,' he motioned to the space between them, 'isn't what you need to be doing.'

Beth stood up; rage coursed through her body. She jumped up the ladder and out of the room in a few steps.

'Hey,' she heard him call, but she was already running out of the shed. 'Beth! Where are you going?' She heard him and it made her happy to hear the panic in his voice. She wanted him to be sorry.

Outside it was already dark and the half-moon hung like a fingernail clipping. She ran towards the tower.

She climbed up to the first landing, then the second, higher and higher. Her fast, angry steps banged out across the night, across the paddocks and the town. She couldn't see how high she was and she didn't care.

She climbed the final spindly ladder that led to the office chair, then she swung herself up and onto it. She spun around, leaning back, pushing with her feet, feeling the night air blow into her face. The lights of the town blurred into one small smear of light. She kept spinning until she felt dizzy and had to grip tightly on the armrests. She stopped the chair with her feet but everything kept on spinning. When the spinning finally stopped she could see all the way to the horizon. There was still a faint line of light from where the sun had gone down. She could see the refinery and the town; it looked pretty, pretty like a fairytale, but impermanent, like if she just breathed out it would all disappear. She held her breath and looked over at her mother's house.

It was just one tiny light to the left of the town site. The kitchen light. She wondered if her mother would even look for her if she never went back to that house, she wondered if she was worried now. She exhaled. From up there she could see how much she hated that house. She wished it would just disappear. Beth closed her eyes and imagined her mother's house gone, the whole town gone. All swept up and done away with. Even the man and his farm and all his preparations – gone. From up there she imagined herself watching it all happen, everything below her being covered by a tsunami or some kind of giant twister or a nuclear blast – anything that would completely obliterate it. From up here she would like to watch that. From up here she would be the last remaining survivor.

The Ascension

Carrie didn't have any kind of visa to stay in the country. Her tourist visa had run out six months before. So she ended up working for cash at her new friend Marianne's New Age bookstore. That was where she met Bruce. Twice a week he came in to do healing sessions in the back room and sell his book, *A Human Being's Guide to Ascension*.

On their first meeting Bruce began by telling her a number of things about herself. The first thing he said was: 'Stop running. You won't be happy until you stop running.'

Carrie kind of agreed. She had been thinking the same thing herself for a number of years. Running had been the proper response at one point but not anymore. Two weeks later she moved in with him.

Bruce lived in a neat fibro house on the main street of a wheat and sheep town. Once, his parents had owned the entire town and all the land surrounding. When they died they left it to Bruce, their eldest son.

Bruce was extremely good looking. Carrie thought he looked like one of the male models in a John Deere billboard she passed every day on her way to work. He was tall and tanned and had all the chiselled masculine angles that were considered attractive. Carrie felt there was something untrustworthy about such good looks, but she supposed he couldn't really help that and he had a nice place, neat and clean. It felt like the perfect place to stop running.

The first night, he ran her through his 'end times prophesies'. He explained that they were living in the last days, that society was coming to an end and only those who were pure enough, and had done the spiritual work, would ascend to heaven. He even had a date for all this to occur: the twelfth of the twelfth 2012, a month away.

That first night, he sat under a reading lamp on the other side of the lounge room. It was strange, Carrie thought, that he didn't want to get close or make any sexual advances. He had asked her to move in with him and she had agreed, under the assumption that he was attracted to her and that they would begin a sexual relationship. Instead Bruce talked on for hours; there seemed no end to his doomsday monologue, he hardly took a breath, let alone the time to make any moves. He explained that in a past life he had been Jesus Christ of Nazareth. 'I was born Jewish, saw the error of the Jewish faith and began preaching the message of loving kindness from the age of thirty.' He spoke in a sharp monotone, matter-of-fact, as if someone had asked him about drenching sheep or the ins and outs of combine harvesters.

At first she thought that the ascension he spoke of represented some sort of internal enlightenment or transcendence of the mind. But soon he was unfolding diagrams of bodies ascending to the heavens, pictures of corpses rising from tombs. There were abstract blue celestial beings, there were photocopies of newspaper articles – the US invasion of Afghanistan, China's nuclear arms – all highlighted and sticky-noted, all fulfilment of prophesy as put forth in the well-worn, gilt-edged Book of

Revelation, which he also kept close at hand on the side table.

'You see,' he pointed to a chronological list of political events, 'You see, it's all here – you can see it, can't you?'

Carrie nodded. His eyes were glistening and intent behind his reading glasses; he had his leg folded over like he was a real scholar. Carrie's instinct was to laugh, but she held it back. His cheeks glowed pink, as if he was about to burst with the sheer joy of sharing his monumental findings. Staring down at the swirling carpet between them, Carrie thought: everyone carried on with such a lot of bullshit in life, why was his bullshit any worse than all the others? At least he'd done his research.

At about eleven at night Carrie yawned. 'So what do I need to do?' she asked. 'Like, to ascend?'

'Believe,' he whispered energetically. 'All you have to do is believe what I'm saying is true.'

That seemed easy enough. She had believed all sorts of flawed ideology in her life, like the notion that hard work paid off. She had believed in friendships and family, in trust and loyalty, she had even believed in 'The One'. At thirty-nine, she often had trouble committing to many generally accepted social concepts. But she thought if she put her mind to it, it might work.

Carrie asked if he had any wine; she usually drank a bottle a night. Bruce informed her that they must remove all defilements – there was no time for distracting diversions or self-indulgence if they were to work towards ascension. He explained that she would have to follow his strict raw food, no-sugar diet. No chocolate or wine for her. In fact, there would be a lot of fasting over the next few weeks. This, Carrie realised, was going to be the hardest part.

At midnight Bruce showed her to the spare room he had

prepared for her. The room smelt of fresh paint, and the crisp pink and yellow bedsheets she could tell were brand new. She didn't know whether to feel relieved or rejected when he said goodnight abruptly and shut the door. On the bedside table was a fresh bunch of white daisies in a glass vase. She lay down and watched the water in the vase tremble slightly with the sound of a distant beat. She had heard it earlier. It must have been coming from the pub down the road. She closed her eyes and fell asleep quickly.

∗∗∗

She didn't find out until a week later that everyone in town called him 'The Jesus Guy'. They were at the annual agricultural show where Bruce had a stand doing palm readings and healing sessions. Bruce had bailed up the man selling chilli jam a few stalls down.

'Yup, died on the cross, all of that,' Bruce had said. 'Paid for *your* sins.' He pointed his finger right into the man's chest as he talked, just in case the man thought he hadn't died for him specifically. The man laughed and Bruce said, 'Oh you laugh. You laugh because you know it's true!'

Carrie, sitting at the stall, felt herself slide down in the chair, hiding behind the piles of Bruce's pamphlets and books. She watched a local woman walking past turn to her friend and say, 'Jesus is at it again.' The friend shook her head and rolled her eyes in a weary rebuff, a mannerism Carrie felt some affinity with.

She sat at the stall as the heat rallied against her, wondering what she'd gotten herself into. She fantasised about secretly buying a hot dog and an ice-cream, but she was just too exhausted by the heat, and the lack of a decent meal, to move. It seemed the town was already taking a toll on her. For the first week it had been radiant. So completely opposite to everything she'd ever known at home in Europe. She thought, how could a place like this exist? That humans inhabited it, exhilarated her.

After this first week the intensity of the heat seemed to bore holes in her eyeballs. She blinked and squinted, her eyes red and weepy. She had to wear sunglasses constantly. When she opened her mouth, flies entered. Words came out hard and blunt and gravelly. Her face seemed to change shape just from looking at it all. Nothing new came or went in that town. The wheat fields all around were yellow seas, shimmering with white heat like they could morph into giant fireballs right before her eyes. She started to think maybe the world was ending, maybe these were in fact the last days.

On the second week they went to the saleyards to sell off the lambs. Bruce had disappeared and she was looking for him when a man approached.

'Listen,' he said. He talked loudly and his hot tobacco breath charged at her face. 'I dunno what your story is but I'm Bruce's brother.'

'Oh, it's nice to meet you, I didn't know ...' she began.

'You know he's completely out of his mind. You know that, don't you? We have to call the mental health unit every other week to come and take him away. Guy's a fucking nut job.'

The brother barely looked at her as he talked, preferring to squint over the top of her head. Like Bruce, he was tall and sunburnt. The only difference she noted was the beginning of a beer gut under his khaki work shirt.

Before she even knew how to respond he was walking away. 'Anyway, I'm through with the prick.' He threw his hands up, already three or four paces from her. 'He won't take his meds, won't see the psych, this time he's Jesus, last time it was bloody Hitler! Christ!'

Bruce's brother disappeared into the sales office. Carrie felt shrivelled and stupid leaning against the steel railing of the sheep pens, her mouth still open in surprise despite the marauding flies.

Later in the afternoon she lay on her bed and tried to focus on her breathing. The meditation sessions Marianne ran at lunchtime in the store often made her feel more relaxed. They stopped her mind running away. That was the thing, she could stop running, but her mind – that was a different matter. Her mind was constantly in movement, trying to solve, fix, plot, pre-empt. She tried to slow it down. What was she feeling? Anger? Anger that Bruce had turned out to be a lunatic? Anger that she had thrown herself at *any port in a storm,* once again?

She let out a deep breath. She had to say something to him. She had to have the courage to act differently, not act out of fear or some other emotion. She remembered something she had read in the book Marianne had given her: 'It's never too late to have a happy childhood.' It was never too late to live outside the shadow of the past; she'd be forty next year and this kind of behaviour could just go on and on forever.

He came in from harvesting, glistening. Sometimes he looked so perfect, like he was straight out of a commercial. That's what he was – a commercial for life, not the real thing. She felt ripped off, then angry at herself for being so presumptuous.

'I wanted to talk to you.' She got up from the bed and came out to the kitchen.

'Talk? This isn't the time. We need to pray, and clean up.' He looked around the house. Her butter and knife were still out on the kitchen bench. She'd bought a loaf of bread in secret, eating the whole thing in one afternoon.

Carrie felt puffs of silence leave her mouth. She wasn't very good at this; initiating dialogue wasn't her thing. After all, how do you ask someone if they are crazy? She heard the shower turn on before she realised she was standing by herself in front of the kitchen bench.

That night she tried to justify her staying. Lying in bed, she told herself she was getting used to the silence, enjoying it even. What better way to realise the important things in life than to partake in a countdown to the end of it?

At three in the morning Carrie decided to pack her bags. Enough with the false bravado, she thought, it was the best thing for both of them. Putting her belongings in the case she felt she was doing a good service, being dutiful. This was the one thing she knew how to do – leave – and she did it as efficiently and wordlessly as a night-shift worker knocking off.

But this time she hadn't thought it through. There was no way to get out of town, no buses or trains. All she could do was steal his car. But she thought – from working with Marianne, who was always going on about having integrity – that stealing should be beneath her. She'd been keeping a tally on all the immoral things she'd done and at her age it was pretty disturbing.

She sat on the suitcase and considered what she really wanted in life. What would it all look like in five years time? Often she tried to imagine a toddler, but she found anything to do with raising children tedious and draining. Her mind went to the other women in town; some of them had lived in the same place for twenty, thirty, sixty–odd years. The thought of staying in one place for that long sickened her. What if she made the decision to stay here for three years? It felt like death, or a death of something.

The sun started to come up and she began unpacking everything again. She was busy folding her clothes and putting them back in the drawer when she noticed Bruce at the door, his face still puffed up with sleep.

'What are you doing?' he whispered. He wore chequered pyjamas that were too big for him.

'Just tidying up,' she smiled.

***

She talked to Marianne at the bookstore the next day.

'I don't think it's going to work out,' she blurted out, 'with Bruce.'

'Do you love him?' Marianne asked, rearranging the crystals on the front counter.

'I don't know.' Those kind of pie-in-the-sky questions always annoyed her. 'I can't pin down emotions like that. I just wanted a place to think about my next move. That's all.' She didn't want to tell Marianne that she thought Bruce was crazy with the whole Jesus thing. She wondered if Marianne already knew that, and, if she did, why she hadn't warned her. 'I just needed something to look forward to, I guess. I've read about that type of condition. The reward centre of your brain has been overstimulated in some way and it never quite calms down, always looking for something to hope for, some incentive, some prize, some promise of reward. Maybe I took too much ecstasy when I was younger, I don't know. Maybe I should be on antidepressants or something.'

'Maybe it's just being human,' Marianne said.

It felt like Bruce was some kind of reward. When she first met him, straight away her brain had started hatching little plots and devising schemes to get him to notice her. The two weeks before she moved in were really the peak of the relationship – those two days a week when he came in to do spiritual healing and sell his guidebook. Those two days, she had dressed differently, she became a different person, a better person, someone she liked a whole lot more.

'Somewhere along the line, though,' she said to Marianne, 'I got the idea that my purpose is to keep moving. I don't like to get bored,' she adjusted the letters on the label-maker, 'but, I suppose, more than that, I don't want to be boring. I want to be the interesting one at parties.'

'Don't we all,' Marianne said. Then she stopped what she was doing and smiled. 'Sometimes you have to just trust that things will unfold as they should. Don't try to think, or do – just be, just sit with it all a while.'

Carrie felt tears well up. She swallowed hard and focused on the labelling of the incense sticks.

Carrie had never had a long-term relationship. Some of her dalliances had definitely had potential but she had never stayed long enough to find out. The first argument or sign of trouble and she was out the door. She always left first, like it was some kind of competition, a running race. She'd always beat them, getting out while they were at work or asleep.

At the end of the fourth week, he hired the town hall and put an ad up in the shop window: *The Coming Apocalypse and What to Expect.* He stuck it in between an advert for a combine harvester and a handwritten *Hay Bales For Sale* sign. Carrie gave him some options for wording it differently. 'Maybe just invite people for a catch-up and a coffee,' she said. 'Have something a little friendlier, less Doomsday.' But Bruce said people needed the truth and there was no need for diluting it.

Nobody showed up, of course. The inside of the town

hall looked like it had been untouched since 1963. It smelt like wheat and dust and her modern jeans and sneakers seemed to juxtapose its very being. Carrie tried to busy herself making a cup of tea and looking at the old photos on the walls, of the town's celebrated farmers and football players. One of them she recognised as Bruce's brother.

'I met him,' she pointed to the photo. 'Your brother, I met him at the saleyards last week.'

Bruce was silent.

'You didn't tell me you had a brother.' Carrie took a sip from her too-hot tea.

'He's not my brother.'

'What do you mean? You're obviously related. You look alike.'

'He's no brother. He tried to silence me; man's a heretic. They have ears but they do not hear.'

Carrie could hear the shudder in his voice but she was tired of the charade.

'Well, I have eyes and I can see. Something isn't right here.'

'Something isn't right with me?'

'I don't know, all I see is a lot of people ...' He looked hurt and she wanted to backtrack, but she felt she'd talked herself into a corner. 'A lot of people think you're crazy.'

This wasn't the conversation she wanted to be having. She felt bad – there was something so genuine and shy about his mannerisms, the way he scratched his arm thoughtfully with his index finger and pursed his lips coyly.

'I'm no false prophet. I want them to see the truth, that's all. I'm not interested in making friends.'

Carrie nodded.

'You believe my brother?'

'No ... sometimes I just wonder why you don't have any followers besides me.'

He put his pamphlets on the table, then went over and put both hands on her shoulders.

'You're the only follower I need,' he said.

After an hour of waiting she left. Starving, she was intent on going past the town shop and pigging out on potato chips. Stepping out into the blazing afternoon sun, she glimpsed back to see him slumped in the plastic chair, one man in a giant hall, a big man made small. Pity was what she probably felt and she immediately regretted it. It was never good to pity someone – not good for them, not good for her. She wondered if that was one of the reasons she felt compelled to stay.

She hadn't been home for five minutes when there was a knock at the flyscreen door.

From the silhouette she thought it was Bruce back already, but as she walked closer she saw his brother.

He gave a loud sigh. 'I've been talking to the mental health nurses from Meckering. Bruce hasn't taken his medication for three months now.' He put his fist on the handle of the door. 'Can you let me in or what?'

Carrie hesitated. Her illegal immigrant status has been on her mind the past few days, plus it didn't really feel like her house to let people into. But she wanted to find out more about Bruce, and the brother – with his self-assured swagger – was hard to say no to. She flicked the latch.

'They're all worried he's gonna do something,' the brother continued. 'Thing is, you mighta cottoned on by now, Bruce is a paranoid schizophrenic. These are his pills.' He shook them up near his ear in a gesture that was patronising, then slapped the box of tablets on the kitchen bench. He took a distracted breath at the kitchen then headed back to the front door, shouting, 'Now if he wants to go crucify himself to a light pole I don't give a shit, but I promised the nurse I'd give 'em to him, because I'm meant to be his *designated carer.*'

Once again, Carrie felt speechless and before she had time to respond he was out the door.

It was the tenth of December, which meant there were two days until Ascension Day. Carrie took the box of pills from the bench. It had a bright orange design and various warning stickers. She opened the lower cupboard and carefully hid the box behind an old crockpot at the back. She noticed again the beat in the distance, coming from the pub. It was Friday night.

She didn't hear Bruce enter the house; he was so quiet, padding in slowly like he was sneaking up on her. When she looked up from the book she was reading in the lounge room, she jumped at the sight of him. It was dark and the only light came from the small floor lamp next to her.

He looked like a cardboard cutout of himself – no buoyancy or life, just a representation of a man. In the low light his face was shadowy and sunken, full of dips and curves, like all the skin was clinging hard to his face.

'Are you okay?' Carrie asked.

He stared at a point in the kitchen, wide-eyed, transfixed. He couldn't seem to hear her. Carrie got up from the armchair. Not until she was only a few steps from him did he register her presence. He flinched like he'd just noticed a projectile approaching his face.

'I need to take a shower.' He turned and went towards the bathroom.

Carrie wanted to follow him, but instead she said, 'I'll make you some food.' For once he didn't protest.

She made the coleslaw that he had made her on the

first night she stayed with him. Listening as the shower turned on, she opened the cupboard and reached behind the crockpot. She broke one of the capsules then sprinkled its contents over his bowl.

The next day she hid another pill in the green juice that he always drank in the mornings.

Usually he slept only a few hours, staying up all night poring over his Bible, scanning religious magazines and taking notes. Sometimes he prayed in supplicating, head-shaking murmurs. But on the evening of the eleventh, at half past ten, Bruce fell asleep, on the couch, under a pile of *Prophecy Watch* magazines. He looked so peaceful that Carrie put a blanket over him and went to bed herself.

Just after midnight, light flooded her bedroom. There was shouting – so loud – like someone was in the room with her, like their face was rested on the pillow next to hers and they were shouting into her face.

She jumped out of bed with her hands to her ears.

'Bruce! Bruce!' a booming loudspeaker voice shouted.

Then she realised it was coming from outside.

'We're still here, mate!' There was laughing and a car horn beeping. 'The blue men haven't taken us away!' More over-the-top drunken laughter came rising, kookaburra-like, through the window. An engine revved and wheels spun in the gravel of the driveway. 'We're still fuckin' here, Bruce!'

She recognised one of the drunken deep-throat laughs as belonging to Bruce's brother. Carrie ran to the window but couldn't see out for the blinding spotlights. She ran down the hallway and saw that Bruce was standing in the middle of the lounge room in his boxer shorts. She rushed past him to the window to see a ute pull away, all its spotlights shining across the paddocks like daylight.

Swaying men, some holding stubbies, were silhouetted on the tray at the back of the ute. One of them held a loudspeaker.

Nothing was said the next day. Bruce only came out of his room to get a glass of water around seven a.m., his brows furrowed. He was chewing his bottom lip. She watched him from her bed as he went down the hallway back to his room. At about nine a.m. she got up and knocked on his door. There was no sound and she turned the doorknob to find him lying on his back on the bed, completely still, his eyes wide open. She had to watch his chest intently to see the rise of his breath and decide he wasn't dead. Slowly she tiptoed into the room and climbed across the bed. She lay down next to him and hugged him tight and he didn't try to stop her.

Nadine Browne

Mihaela Nicolescu

Mihaela Nicolescu was born in Romania, brought up in Sweden, and then spent thirteen years in London, where she completed her MA in Creative Writing at Birkbeck College, University of London. She now lives in Perth, Western Australia. Mihaela's short stories have been published in *Mslexia*, *The Mechanics' Institute Review*, *Aesthetica Magazine* and *The New Writer*, and her plays have been produced by Parrabbola and Total Beast Theatre, and as part of London's Off Cut Festival. She was guest editor for three issues of the World Arts Platform publication *Write from the Heart*, celebrating the work of writers who use English as a second language. The stories that appear in this volume were shortlisted in the 2014 City of Fremantle T.A.G. Hungerford Award.

Acknowledgements

Firstly, all my gratitude and love to the two main characters of my life: Muțu and Tuțu. *Mulțumesc pentru încredere și dragoste.* Secondly, thanks to VP, for bringing me to the sunshine and for helping me find my voice. Thirdly, thank you to the friends who have been there, through thick and thin. And finally, Linkwest: thank you ladies (past and present) for providing kindness, lively debate, and insight. I would also like to acknowledge Fremantle Press for giving a gal a break, and for being that most elusive type of animal: a truly professional, considerate, and broadminded publisher.

The following stories have appeared elsewhere: 'Drop', *Petrichor – Visible Ink 27* (RMIT University, Melbourne 2015); 'Frozen', *Eunoia Review* (eunoiareview.wordpress. com/2013/03/14/frozen/); 'Love', *Eunoia Review* (eunoiareview.wordpress.com/2013/03/13/love-3/), *Aesthetica Creative Works Annual 2011* (Aesthetica Magazine, London 2010); 'Fig', *JotSpeak* recording (jotspeak.com, 2010); 'Frozen', *The Mechanics' Institute Review 7* (Birkbeck University, London, 2010); and 'Strays' (titled 'Coiled'), *The Mechanics' Institute Review 2* (Birkbeck College, London, 2005).

Nadine Browne

Nadine Browne was raised as a born-again Christian and wound up an agnostic studying theology at Monash University. Her writing has appeared in numerous publications including *Westerly* and *Antipodes*. She has also been featured on the ABC's *Conversations with Richard Fidler*, *The Moth* (Los Angeles) and *Porchlight* (San Francisco). In her spare time she attends and facilitates a group at the Katharine Susannah Prichard Writers' Centre in the Perth hills. She lives in Perth with her partner Krzysztof and a Pomeranian named Bob.

Acknowledgements

Big thanks to my fellow writers at KSP's Thursday Night Group who have given valuable critique and feedback on all of my stories in this collection. Special thanks to Chris Oakeley for his on-call Grammar Nazi services and general enthusiasm for my writing. Thanks also to Rachel Bailey for being a comrade-in-arms in the battle against creative angst. And thanks especially to my partner Krzysztof Piotrowicz for his patience, kindness and humour.

The following stories have appeared elsewhere: 'Strange Fruit', *Westerly*, July 2012, vol. 57 (UWA Press, WA); 'The Jerry Can', *PiF Magazine*, September 2015 (online edition, Washington, USA); 'The Spiral', *SALA: Short Stories From around Australia*, September 2015 (Extempore Press, Victoria); 'Drowning', F*ourW Twenty Six: New Writing*, November 2015 (Active Print, NSW).

Also from Fremantle Press

available from fremantlepress.com.au